# Paveewhack

## a novel

**PETER BRADY**

was born in 1944 in County Offaly, where he lives with his wife, Katherine. He has three grown-up children, Brigid, Neil and Annie. He works as an assistant principal with County Offaly VEC. *Paveewhack* is his first novel.

# Paveewhack

a novel

PETER BRADY

NEW
ISLAND

**Pavee Whack**
First published October 2001
by New Island Books
2 Brookside
Dundrum Road
Dublin 14

ISBN 1 902602 63 3

British Library Cataloguing in Publication Data. A catalogue
record for this book is available from the British Library.

**The Arts Council**
An Chomhairle Ealaíon

New Island received financial assistance from The Arts Council
(An Chomhairle Ealaíon), Dublin, Ireland.

Cover design: Slick Fish Design
Cover photograph: Pat Langan
Printed in Ireland by Colour Books Ltd.

# Acknowledgements

First, I wish to express my gratitude to The Irish Travellers' Movement, Tullamore, for its advice, suggestions and support in writing this book, and for giving the finished work its approval.

To the writers' group in Tullamore for its encouragement. My thanks in particular to Geraldine, her husband Mike, and Pauline for their assistance and suggestions throughout. Also to the two Johns and Larry, whose colourful expressions breathed life into these fictitious characters.

To Jonathan Williams, my agent, who was adventurous enough to choose this manuscript from his pile, and take the chance, and make some valuable suggestions.

To the people from the midlands and west of the Shannon – thanks for your sayings, anecdotes and colourful speech.

Finally, to Malcolm Ross McDonald, eminent novelist, who unstintingly gives two hours of his time free each fortnight. He's the catalyst, the guru, and without whom this book would never have been written. Thanks Malcolm!

*For John Brady (1910-85)*
*and Rita Brady, neé McEvoy (1913-93)*

# Preface

They tell me the Traveller's life isn't easy. Most the ones I know have settled and they say they enjoyed the road. In my opinion they're viewing their past through rose-tinted glasses.

My parents were Travellers too – until they moved into the town in the mid-Seventies. Four years of age I was then – too young to realise how hard they were finding it to adjust.

Being one of the settled generations, I didn't find settling easy living either. Despite a fair deal of barracking in national school, I survived pretty well. Get on with it has always been my motto. You'll never get anywhere carrying a chip on your shoulder.

It was in secondary school that I really came into my milk. Five years of fitful study and luckily I came good in my exams – enough to pick up a third-level grant.

This would be all uncharted territory for the like of us, seeing I'm the first in our extended family to finish second level, let alone getting to a teachers' training college.

After qualifying in 1994 I find a teaching job in Tullamore, County Offaly, the county of my birth. There I meet my future wife – a true buffer, and another national school teacher, working in the same school. After a grand wedding, me and my gorgeous laying hen settle into our fine detached four-bedroom two-storey house in the Whitehall Estate.

We've since become proud parents of three young strapping sons, so how far from the travelling tradition can a guy get? Still it's hard to block the urge to travel from the blood. Every spring I feel a twitch.

With regard to my own heritage I'd be far too proud to want to suppress it. Confront your past and you'll be richer for it spiritually, I've always contended. For many years I nurtured an ambition to record the tales of members of my own tribe but I kept putting it on the long finger. A few characters I had in mind – one was a distant uncle by the name of Jack Joyce, affectionately known as Whack. A number of relations had urged me not to miss the opportunity of getting him on tape.

It was only when he'd taken ill I made a resolution to go see him in hospital and even so I mightn't have gone had I not received a message from a cousin that he wanted to see me urgently. Without further ado I headed for the Mullingar General where he lay in a private ward. Apparently his well-heeled cousins were taking good care of him. More about them later.

A fine frame of a man in his prime, and unusual for one from the travelling tradition, he wore a fine head of blond hair and had dazzling blue eyes. Imagine my alarm when I saw him lying there, worn down to skin and bone, looking every day of his fifty-three years and a lot more years besides.

They doin tests come Monday, he says, reading the initial shock of alarm on my face. As if they don't know already, but I can assure ya, Pecker Joyce, I is not feelin one bit hopeful.

That's for God to decide.

If ya want me opinion He already have. Anyway they tell me you's interested in recordin the Travellers' ways an customs in the auld times?

I tell him I was hoping to gather recordings and write them in the vernacular at a later stage, similar to the way the Irish Folklore Commission had done in the 1930s, when the Travellers' folklore was faithfully recorded.

I has a story, Pecker, an it be weighin heavy on me mind for ages. Sure hasn't I been rehearsin it for the pasht thirty year in all them places where I be stuck. If I war any good at the scribblin, sure I woulda wrote it down meself ages ago. It mostly concern the time we move intiv the town in the spring a 1960. I can tell ya rakes too about animals – tales about eatin, drinkin, moochin, footballin, fightin, matin – killin even. Most of it really havin to do wuth what happen to me in the helm back in the time when I'm fourteen. That why I aks ya to come, Pecker. Not bein much in the line of a believer meself, there's a few things I'd like to get off me chest fore I kick the bucket like – some little dark secrets I want to get out in the open – things I need to share rather than bring tiv the grave on me own. Ya get me meanin? Suppose we look on it as me last confession fore I depart this mortal life, an you is me cuinnic, Pecker.

Not at all! You mustn't think like that, I say. But my voice lacked conviction.

We arranged a session for the following afternoon. What follows is an unabridged version of Whack's tale related to me over the space of three weeks during that dismal summer of 1998.

# 1

I'm not bullin you, Pecker, but the day me da decide to move hus all in wuth the mushes in the helm me life start to go haywire.

Tisn't some'hin he done off the top of his head, like. A lot of it have to do wuth the Husseys – me granny's kin gettin a council house in the terrace and they persuadin him to move in next dure, an when the truth be told me mother an the granny use a lot of their charms too.

Still I know what me da really think of this whole racket for I remember him tellin me he'll never live within the four grey walls of a cean. He get stuck in Marboro Jail one time for rabusin the shadogs an it put him off settlin. Starin at the wall all day frettin. Not even a dacent windie to look outa, which put me to wonderin how long he stay in this feckin auld kip of a cean in the terrace.

Anaways I come to guessin the rale reason why he move. Sure he be fightin a mighty battle wuth the traipe. First he take the pledge to drink two pints a week but that only give him a taste for scullin a rake more so he couldn't keep tiv that class of promise. The only cure's to keep off it for good, Pecker, that's what I always say. One day at a time's aisier said than done, an aisier done in spring an summertime when the days is long and the weather's kind, an he have things to occupy his mind.

But winter's a hoor of a time wuth short days an long nights an freezin weather. He begin to get itchy round the molly an ruz many's the row, the same buck, an then he'd feck off for himself down tiv the gat cean an back intiv the thick a the drinkin. I suppose he couldn't help it – the poor auld gomey. One night I remember him wobblin back intiv the camp the shoulders of his jacket in tatters, done in from him knockin constant agin the pebble dashin on the walls long the narrow streets up from the helm.

Movin intiv the cean's some'hin I'm not mad about neither, I can tell ya. Ever since the day I be born back in 1945 I been travellin, an at the age a fourteen I'm too fond of the road an too set in me ways to want to settle in wuth a crowd a stuck up buffshams. Still, me best pal, Goat's Tail Hussey, me cousint an a lad me own age move intiv the helm, an I'm sorely missin him.

Travelled round a fair few counties in those days. Still, we ushta keep round Offaly country mostly.

*Wance, and vera good times they was, an twas neither your time nor mine, whin turkeys chewed tobacca an swallas bilt deir nests in auld min's beards.* That's how me dad ushta get them grand auld yarns rollin an he full tiv the gills wuth dreepers a traipe.

You got to be forward-lookin in yer livin, Pecker, but she can only be understood from the pasht, so it's wuth me poor da that I begin me story – this very proud feen from the helm a Tuam be the name of Jim Blocker Joyce.

Back in '34 he marrit Cait McDonagh from the County Mayo – somewhere near Baal – an she give birth tiv me in the spike in Tellamore of a snowy February night in 1945. The McDonaghs – they's all over Ireland in every county an me ma's related tiv nearly everyone a them. Sure ya know that, Pecker.

Jack they call me after me late grandfather Joyce, but I can't get me tongue round that monicker growin up, so they call me Whack, which be the way I pronounce it. As a boy I is gorgeous-lookin, unless them photos is tellin lies, wuth dimples in me cheeks an a big broad smile an a grand nopper a blondy curdles.

Also, I be a hoor for blatherin, so me ma she often call me Blatherwhack.

Me da mushta make every sorta job ever done be a pavee, tho' his big demon's the traipe, but fair plays tiv him, he wake up in earnest after Paddy's Day from a long winter's sleep an start round May wuth cuttin an haypin turf, an me out helpin, an you wouldn't find the summer stealin over ya.

An then come winter again he pass the time wuth the tin. Sure isn't that what we's famous for an called after? Tinkerin round wuth tin he ushta love it boh'omin auld buckets an things makin cans an saucepints an we'd sell them round Westmeath an Offaly mostly.

But the times for the Travellers be changin. For the dole you need a steady address. The chin wag me da have wuth the Puckeen Hussey – me uncle, a bare knuckle boxin champion for the whole thirty-two counties of Ireland – in his council house in the terrace have no small bearin on his movin in, I reckon.

I'd brought a ferret up tiv Goat's Tail, the Puckeen's son, an this is what I hear them argue.

It's nearly time ya considered settlin, Block, me uncle say tiv him outa the blue. The days of the tin's well gone.

Yea, plastic's all the go now, says me da. Sure any auld gomey knows that, an praggs is nearly all gone as well.

The tractor's the fella now, an I hear donkeys is bein made intiv dog mate.

An cullions is bein took up by machines. So ya can throw yer spade in the ditch now, Blocker, an cuttin turf wuth the slean's nearly a thing a the past too.

So's peddlin from dure to dure.

An the conies is riddled wuth the myxie.

We may go shoot ourselfs, me da's sayin now in despair.

Or move intiv the town like hus, Block.

There's no way I'm goin in there.

An why not?

Them auld mushes in the helm 'id do yer head in. That's so. Cause we never reared to be settled, Puck. We's been travellin the tober for generations, an it's not aisy give up at this stage at our age. If yer a travellin man there's only one road ta travel.

Well we's been livin on clippins a tin for centuries, an I've come tiv the end a that particular road. It's time to move on, boy.

Well, ya know another reason why I hate goin intiv that auld helm, Puck?

The shadogs?

Aye, especially that auld Sargint Gillick. If you was to rake hell's coals an riddle the cinders you wouldn't find a rottener bastard, an he after sendin me to prison for bein drunk an disorderly five year ago to say nothin bout batin the livin shite outa me ten million time. I'm sure he an his pals they'd love ta see the likes a Jim Blocker Joyce movin intiv his patch. When yer livin on the wrong side of the tracks there's shag all differ between right an wrong in their eyes, Puck.

Sure that's all in the past. I've no trouble since settlin. Keep yer bib clean. That's all ya have to do.

That's grand comin from the likes a you an ya smugglin stuff in an outa the north no bother whenever ya please.

Sure, but the trick's not to get caught.

Wait til your time come, we'll see what fun you knock outa goin to law wuth them divils an the court held in hell.

Don't be so down on yerself.

Let me aks ya, what's to be got outa livin in the helm?

Loads a runnin water, a warm fire, a tilet. All the comforts you'll be missin on the road. Scrap's aisier got an the gat cean's aisier to get inta.

What about me plans for the horses an I movin in there?

Rent the long acre, an work it out wuth the Man above. By the yard or the mile – I hear His terms is very reasonable. Look, Jim, the house next tiv hus is empty. Go intiv the council an aks straigh away. You'll be able to draw the dole from that address along wuth a few more I'll give you.

Without puttin too much of a tooth in it I'm not on for your crooked ways, Puckeen Hussey.

Well that's me advice tiv ya now. Take it or leave it.

Of course he say nothin about losin yer freedom when you move intiv a cean, or how the Puck, himself, misses the road. I've a fair notion what me uncle want – a feelin he's lonely for his own, an he's cravin for me da to move next dure so they can chat an drink together. So I might as well tell ye I'm not one bit happy when he finally take tiv that arrangement, but me granny's delighted as well as the ma, an me sister, Ribleen.

## 2

On the furst day we move intiv the cean, Goat brings me on a tour of the helm, not that I need it cause I mooch there many's the time before an know it inside out, an I gets to know a good few of that crowd, some even better than Goat do.

Standin at her dure as usual an we leavin the terrace is that awful auld heart-scald, the Widda Mooney, the nosy auld witch, an we's no choice but to pass her an say hello an try to brave her viper tongue.

Goat starts hummin:

*Chickety chock aroun the rock.*
*I sold me buttermilk every drop*
*An if I had more*
*I'd sell it in score*
*An that's the way the buttermilk go.*

There before hus is her pet dog hunkered in the gutter – his back arched in the middle of doin his business.

You'd think the townies would do a better job mindin their pets, Goat shouts out for her to hear. The dog leaves behind what looks like a lump a white madder you see out on the bog.

You'd suppose they'd feed them some'hin more than bones, I says, getting in me own little dig.

Things isn't what you suppose, says the auld cow. Still I'll

17

bet ya it's more than ye feed yer own, the auld witch says contradictin herself. Sure, isn't it after the dogs ye get yer manners, shittin in fields, on the roads, or wherever ye feel like to get it outa ye, so get on outa that, ye dirty pair a tramps.

What a lovely neighbour, I says tiv Goat. Every time I pass that poisoned dwarf she have some'hin grand to say bout hus Travellers.

Comin up the hill to his house in the terrace, we meet Joe Joe Meagher lookin like a ghost wuth white dust all over him after the night shift in the flour mill. A dacent auld skin – he'll talk tiv ya at least – not like that other auld stuck-up shower in the helm, Pecker, actin like they's in a different class tiv ourselfs.

Me granny ushta say they don't like to get too close tiv hus cause we keep remindin them where they come from theirselfs. The sight of hus makes them fidgety. Like we cut too close to the bone for their likin, is the very words she use.

And how are our two newcomers taking to their new surroundings this weather? Joe Joe aks hus.

We's been takin nothin only rabuse, I say. The other day an I passin a few buffers on the road, this woman's babby roars, Look at the get-up of the tinker, mammy, an the other evenin in Flynn's me ma goes to get some milk off the shelf. Not there, the auld bitch shouts from across the counter. The tinker's milk's over here!

Jesus, isn't that rich coming from the likes of her an she off a wee farm a rushes herself, Joe Joe says. Many's the time I seen her out in the fields and she up to her ankles in muck in her sawn off wellingtons. She'd be too thick to know any better, son. Ignore the auld sow.

One time before, he tell me how much he hate farmers – that he'd been discriminated upon when he be born. His mother work as a maid for this big quare geezer of a farmer out the country – an odd gint that gets her wuth a babby an then refuse to marra her, cause his auld one wouldn't allow it, so she loses her job and have to go fend for herself wuth not a penny tiv her name. This buffer never get marrit an Joe Joe claims he shoulda inherited that big farm but it go tiv the farmer's nephew instead after he die. A lousy dirty rotten mane shower, he says tiv me. Have nothing to do with them, Whack, an you've my permission any time to go steal all ye can off them – providin you don't get caught. Now tell me, he says then. Who's yer friend here?

That's Jimmy Hussey, I says, but he go be the name of Goat's Tail.

Now I know how you get your own monicker, Whack, but where in God's earth did he come by that one?

To make a long story short, says Goat, I war moochin out be this auld farmhouse one day an there's nobody in an I sees this lovely hen shed out in the haggard, an she's guarded be a puck goat, an findin a lump a bindin twine near the fince I calls him over an ties his tail tiv it, so I jump over an sucks down a rake a lovely fresh eggs. Then I grabs a rake more, an break some – makin it look like a fox done a raid aan it. An whin I tell the story in the molly they starts callin me Goat's Tail.

Clever fella, says Joe. An I suppose you know why the guards cut the tongues outa them foxes the gunmen brings into the barracks?

So they don't bring them back for a second ten pound, says Goat, quick as a flash.

Very cute chap, Joey laughs. Well lads I must skidaddle, best a luck with all the beggin – an we bid him good mornin.

Jesus, Whack, Goat says, I'm short a few deener. What ya

say to moochin the main street? You play the mouth organ an I'll collect wuth me cap an we'll split the mideogs fifty-fifty.

Outside Kenny's pub an across from Brady's supermarket, I starts suckin an blowin on me Hohner. Reels an jigs is what I likes to play the best. Me favourites is The Sally Gardens and The Yalla Tinker, Goat gettin the odd tingle intiv his an for the day that's in it, being a Wednesday – the day before payday in the mill – we's not doin too bad at all at all, Pecker.

I'm well inta The Longford Collector when this rough paw grabs at me shoulder from behint. Next I'm glarin intiv the wild grey oglers of Garda Fitzmaurice.

Cheeky, I ushta call him, cause he can get very sassy wuth ya. Also there's a pair a mighty ones on aitch side of his puss wuth dimples in them when he smile, which be seldom.

Then Goat come up wuth a better idea. Ya ever notice the cheeks on that shadog's puss, he say tiv me one day. Just like two slabs a dead meat, you'd swear they was glued on. Milky white like a pork chop.

That's it! Well done Goat! We'll call him Pork Chops!

You're breakin the law, he says to hus now, begging on this street. Get a move on now, ye pair a tramps, and if I catch ye at this again I'll be landin ye in jail.

This is the second time in about the space of a half-hour we gets called by this name. Off we go then, an hide in the park for a while splittin up the mideogs even between hus.

Why I remember all this? It's cause this day leave a big impression. Me furst time livin among the townies, an I don't feel one bit good about it neither. I'm like a wild animal in a zoo, an the guards is like zoo keepers.

Let's mooch the gat ceans, Goat says tiv me then. I'm bored sittin here. We make feck all deener aan the street. Sure enough it's getting dark, an we stand a fair chance of avoidin Shadog Pork Chops Fitzmaurice.

An we do all right too that evenin, me an Goat. Jesus, if I'd a bowran we'd a made mighty grade, says Goat tiv me later, an he without a note in his head, while I picks it up off the da's side of the family.

That evenin an I gettin home there's a mighty feed waitin for me, an me ma wantin to know where I be, an before I can open me mouth there comes this loud knockin, an before anyone can open the dure or any'hin, Monsignor Diskin's standin fornenst hus in the kitchen. The sight of this tall thin man in his black suit an white shiny dog collar an a black hat coverin his baldy nopper pretty well stuns hus.

The nerve of him to come straigh in without bein aksed, me da keep complainin long after he's left. He must reckon we comes well below him in the peckin order a things.

Me auld granny she have mighty sayins. The two worst pets ye can have, she say winkin at me, is a pet pig an a pet priest. To keep a cuinnic in his place – yer better off not bein too mane nor too nice wuth the gomey.

No sign of him ever comin out to hus in the molly, says me ma.

That's cause he'd end up smellin a sticks.

And it come to pass in those days Caesar Augustus send out a decree that all his subjects should be taxed.

That's how he begin his little spake.

Course we hasn't a clue from Adam what he's aan about til he say that since we's new tiv the parish he want to know a few things about hus. He aks how many childerin's in the family.

Me ma tell him five. He stare at me, Ribleen an Mulchas in his cot, then aks her, Where's the other two?

What business is it tiv you where they is? says me da, getting ratty.

Well done, dad, I'm urgin him on inside me head. Go after that arroghint stuck-up auld cuinnic. Give him plenty a rabuse.

But Diskin's well trained intiv treatin the likes of hus tinkerin folk like dirt, an a man of pride feel no pain when it come to hurtin others.

Oh we need to get some facts for the parish record, he grunts, peerin up from his little notebook where he's been busy writin.

We's two grown sons in England, say me ma, wantin to avoid scandal in any shape or form wuth the super cuinnic.

Were they all baptised? the Monsignor aks rale sharp.

What ya think we's rearin? me da butt in. Heathens, eh?

I never suggested anything of the kind, says the Monsignor, stickin his ruddy nose up in the air. I'm sure you're all good law-abidin and practising Catholics in this house. Do you go to Mass every Sunday yourself, Mister Joyce?

Me granny say, If holy water was whiskey, he'd go every day, Father.

Diskin don't find that a bit funny.

On an on he goes, gettin names, ages, where we's born an baptised, an aksin a whole load of very personal stuff like how often does we go to confession an Communion, does we all go to Mass every Sunday an holy days? He's hopin to build a new chapel an we's expected to put money intiv the fund every week like all the other good dacent servin saps he have under him.

Me da stand there grumblin, while the Monsignor tells hus he's now goin to bless the house an aks hus all to kneel, which we all do, bar me da, an we listen in silence while he starts prayin. Then he gets hus to say an Our Father after him.

22

Before he leave he remind da to be sure an enrol me in the tech for the comin autumn.

The nerve of that black cuinnic, me father say, givin out after he leave, an me a pure pagan. He'll get no deener offa me. An the tech, he says. How come he never mention the Brothers? Is they too good for me son or what?

# 3

Next day Goat bring me down to the river. There's a place I wants to show ya, he say. A nice little spot where nobody know, an whenever we gets inta trouble or wanta meet in secret we can go in here. What's more, I'm the member of a little gang we's just after settin up, an I want ya to join.

What would I want to do that for?

Oh, just for the bit of company an fun. Nothin more. At the minute there's only one more in it long wuth me.

Who's that?

You'll be meetin him shortly.

I follow him along this rough path that leads into some thick undergrowth. After a while we comes to a stone wall that mushta been a yard thick, curvin along til it come to the river bank an runs alongside it, leavin a margin of about four foot of ground. Next it lean out toward the water wuth ivy hangin down from the top. This is the gang's hidin place. She's grand an dry in there, an they have a big tin box at one end.

I aks Goat what's in it.

We get tiv that later, he say. So we sits there listenin to the water gurglin over the rocks. We bend down an look into the river. The water – crystal clear – have minnows an pinkeens an black beetles dartin round underneath.

Jesus Goat, what have ya got in that box? I aks him again.

Just you hauld yer horses, he say. I'm waitin for me pal to appear so we can make you a new member.

Next thing I hear this shufflin thro the bushes an before I can say boo in come Noddy Stokes, another settled Traveller, bout our own age. As to how he get that monicker – furst he's called Neddy, but as a lad he get addicted tiv them Noddy books in the libraries. He ushta love Mister Plod an Big Ears, so they end up callin him Noddy.

I hear a number of stories about this fella, an a lot of people has him down for havin space to rent upstairs. Give me a swig outa that box there, ya mane little bollix, he tell Goat. I'm dyin for a sup of the creatur.

Goat leans over, lift off the lid an pull out a bottle of the hard stuff – a dreeper of poteen he steal off the Puckeen, his father. Next he pull out a glass an half fillin it wuth water outa the river he top it up wuth firewater, an pass it over to Noddy who take a right swig an smack his lips. Then Goat take it from him an do the same, leavin the glass about a quarter full, which he put next tiv the box.

Whin do I get mine? I aks.

Not til we swear you in as a member of the gang furst, Goat says.

Remember, what passes between hus here in this hide must be kept secret. Will you have a problem wuth that, Whacker Joyce? Noddy aks me then.

I've no worries on that score, but I'm more afraid bout one a youse spillin the beans. I mean what's there in this caper to bind hus together?

Furst, we's here to help ourselfs get on in the helm, an to help aitch other get our own back on the shower that runs this town, like some of the guards, teachers, cuinnics, publicans, shopkeepers – all them that likes to make life difficult for hus. Now don't get me wrong, Whacker. I'm not countin them all – just the few rotten eggs in the basket. Hus Travellers – we has our rights too. Anythin that make their life difficult well I's in favour of, an any chance I get I'll show them up for what they is. Is ye game for all that, biys?

No bother, I says – up tiv a point. I not plannin on doin some'hin foolish where I is goin to get caught. I do me thing in me own way, lads.

We'll go along with that, Noddy say. Now, let's get on tiv the ceremony. Goat, get the razor outa the box.

What razor? I aks.

Oh she'll only be just a little nick, Whacker. Say on the tip of yer finger, an we all do the same. Just a teeny drop a blood each an we mix it all up together. Then you swear to keep all our secrets. After that you's a member.

Where ya get this idea, Nod?

In a comic.

Goat give his thumb a nick an hand the blade to Noddy who do the same an hand it to me. I gives a finger a little stab. A simple job. No pain. The three blobs of blood is mixed together an I swear me oath, an fore I knows it I'm a member of the pavee gang.

Fair dues tiv ya, Noddy say, handin the glass for me to drink.

Firewater's the proper name for that tack all right. Jesus, it neer burn a hole in me gullet. Straightaway I can feel it goin tiv me head.

Spot on, I let a little cry outa meself. Now tell me about what kinda craic ye get yerselfs up tiv?

We only goes after people that has it in for hus. Nothin

more than harmless pranks, mind ya – just to bring them down a peg or two. Isn't that it, Goat?

Spot on, Noddy boy.

Now, Goat, remember our last meetin?

About fingerin a townie that's really getting up me nose?

Have you come up wuth someone?

Auld Stacie Williams, the postmistress.

Couldn't a picked better. An awful auld rip.

I remember seein her in me travels. She have a figure on her like a two hundred weight bag a flour with a rope tied round the middle. Above that line her boobs is drooped wuth no sharp shape tiv them. Below the waist she have a pair a hips that move like a pair a trapped dogs fightin in a sack. And talk about ugly! Jesus, you'd swear onetime her face go on fire an someone try to put it out wuth a shovel.

What's there about her that's gettin up yer nose, Goat? I aks.

She have a tongue that put the Widda Mooney's in the shade. Any time me mother go in there to collect the dole she come out wuth some'hin nasty about hus bein Travellers.

Cause she's in charge of the telephone exchange, Nod add, her big pastime is listenin in on all the juicy talk goin on. She even been known to butt in an give her own opinion if she don't like what she's hearin.

Jo Jo Meagher swear she open letters wuth the steam off the kettle, Goat say.

Little wonder she an Sarge Gillick get on so well together, says Noddy. Any time he want some dirt on somebody he call in on Stacie. She sure to have some'hin. Tell me, Whacker. You's hardly two days in the town. Is there anyone in the place yet that's been gettin up yer nose?

Now that you mention it, I suppose the Widda Mooney.

What a surprise, says Nod. She's high on our shit list too. We's already got a little plan for her, hasn't we, Goat?

Surely Ned.

What's that? I aks.

Never mind. All you need do is come tiv next Sunday evenin devotions. Sit up close tiv the front an you'll see for yerself. She won't be likin it neither, will she, Goat?

I'm sure Goat'll tell me bout their little surprise after we say goodbye to Ned on the way into town, but he remain stubborn. That would only ruin it for ya, he say. Pop in next Sunday evenin. Stay well away from me an Ned. An make sure you're there good an early.

# 4

The followin evenin I do what I'm told. Goin out the dure me da aks me where I'm headin. To the devotions, I says, an he bursts out laughin. Don't tell me your granny's puttin you up tiv this?

She have nothin to do wuth it. If she done twould turn me off altogether – what, wuth her quare ways an habits, I says spoutin out the furst things that comes intiv me head.

Then what's got intiv ya to be goin tiv devotions of a lovely Sunday evenin like this when you could be out trainin ponies or learnin Eyebrows to give ya the paw? Or just take a look at Father Sun goin down below the horizon to keep the other side of the ball shiny an warm? If it waren't for Him where would Mother Nature be?

Up shit creek, I say.

The sun's our provider, lad. Them's me beliefs. My advice tiv ya is this. Stay away from that bunch of auld women. They only goes there for the tongue wag. Religion should be a lot more simpler than they're makin it out to be, son. Who need all that red tape from the Vatican anyway?

He's in the depth of his arguin, when I slips out the dure.

I sneak in nice an early for the devotions. The Sacred Host is exposed on the altar, an those comin in is mostly auld women who bow deeply fore getting into their seats. I make me way down the aisle keepin a sharp eye out for the two boys. I see Goat's carrot-coloured head up front but no sign a Noddy. Next I see Joe Joe's big curdly nopper in the pew behind Goat.

I slips in next tiv him.

I hear there's a treat for us this evenin, he whisper in me ear.

Who tauld you?

Your mate the Goat. What kind of prank are ye goin to play on our poor auld friend, Whack?

I is as much in the dark as you, Joe Joe.

Next thing the Widda Mooney comes waddlin in an make straight for the candle holder in front of the little altar to the left. Me an Joe both wonderin what's goin to happen. She put her pennies intiv the slot, pluck two candles out of the drawer underneath an place them in the holders on top. She light one wuth a match an is in the middle of lightin the other when the furst one let off a bang near liftin her head off an singein her eyebrows an hair. She let out a shriek an fall on her back on the flure. Her veiny auld legs shoot up in the air an we can see her baggy blue bloomers. Thanks be to Jesus I don't see beyant them or I woulda fainted.

Well done, Nod, I says tiv meself, wonderin what I just get meself intiv when I goes an joins the Pavee Club. Who's next on our shit list I'm wonderin. Stacie Williams?

\*

In no time the story's all over the place. Now I know why you's so mad to go to the devotions tonight, me da say when I return home. You think I came down in the last shower, son? You want to know some'hin. Gillick will make you his number one suspect. I bet you never think a that!

No, that thought never come to me at all at all.

30

The auld sarge will follow this one up. He's goin to quiz you on it, you can be doubly sure. So you better tell me everythin what happen.

I mention Noddy an Goat an the prank they intend to play, but on me word of honour, I say to me da, I've no idea what the prank's about til it happen. The pair a them keep me in the dark.

Any sign of the two of them in the chapel?

I see Goat all right, but no sign a Noddy.

If a bird was to shit outa the sky twould be sure to land on either one of yer heads. That's cause the two of ye's such a pair a pure gomeys. No fear a Stokes getting caught. He's too clever by half. Son, you better be ready for Gillick, cause he'll try an pin it on you an Goat. Cause of me record he'll try any'hin to nail you. That's the easy way out for the fecker. He don't care what way or means he use. He have a low regard for husses. That much I know. He's more afraid of the Puckeen.

Now you play yer cards rale close. Remember how I show ya how to bluff in poker? He'll be tryin his best to bamboozle you, but you stick tiv yer story. Look how the badger defend himself? Pretend the auld sarghint's a fox hound. He'll be circlin ya, snappin growlin, barkin. What does the badger do?

He get the best grip he can on a leg or the neck an squeeze wuth his jaws – tighter an tighter til he hear a bone crack.

You keep a strong grip on to your side of the story, son. You know how they often tries to cod the badger by snappin a stick, makin him think he just after crackin the hound's bone wuth his teeth, so he'll let go his grip?

Sure.

Well Gillick he try an bluff you into confessin tiv it. He's a evil bastard. He'll try any trick to catch ya, so be rale careful.

Next he start preparin me for the meetin wuth the sarge while I'm all the time hopin twill never come tiv that. But father's right. Sure enough the followin mornin I has a visit from the bollix himself. He pull up outside our dure in a black squad car. The furst thing I notice bout him is his auld grunter's head for the snout's broad an the skin on his puss is pinkish an all, an a pair a big wide ears flappin out under his cap, an there's great tufts of whitish hair growin out of his ears an nose holes.

He get me to sit in, while father give me a wink that say – Remember what I tell you, son. Keep tiv your own story. Deny every'hin else. The barracks is no length away an fore I know it we's sittin facin each other across a plain pine table an he glarin intiv me eyes, tryin his best to make me feel uneasy.

Now lad, he say, I've one simple question. Who put the banger in the candle holder in the chapel?

Haven't a clue, I say. Me breathin's unsteady – me heart poundin away like mad in me ribcage.

And what got into you to go to them devotions in the first place?

I'm goin past the chapel on me own. It's a beautiful sunny evenin. Next I hear this lovely hymn comin from the choir. I feel this spirit or some'hin drawin me in, an that's what I do. I gets into a fit of prayin til this loud bang it near put the heart crossways in me.

And you expect me to believe this from a fella that's never been to devotions before in his whole life. You expect me to swallow that yarn?

Be Jesus you is wrong there boss on both counts.

Be careful how you address me. I'm Sergeant Gillick when I'm in uniform and out of it as well, you young whippersnapper! You were there for a purpose all right, young

32

Joyce, and it sure wasn't for the good of your soul. Now own up to the truth and tell me the real story about why you were there, and hurry up about it cause I don't have all day.

I already tell you the reason I goes in there.

Well I have it from a reliable source that you and the Goat Hussey were involved in this racket along with some others. You may tell me the truth now Joyce or you'll end up like yer old man, in a whole load of trouble.

At this stage I'm not sure whether he's bluffin me or not, and I beginnin to feel confused. Do what your father tell you, this little voice inside me's sayin: Don't stray from your main story. Stick tiv your guns, Whack. You can do no more.

An where did you get that news from? I aks Gillick.

From your neighbour next dure – the Goat himself.

Again this little voice is sayin: Don't fall for that shite.

Well there's someone tellin lies, I say back, an it sure isn't me.

He says ye done it as part of a prank. Come on now, lad, and admit to it.

There's no way I'll admit to some'hin I know nothin about. I'm not even a week in the helm. I know hardly anybody an you's tryin to pin the blame on me. You lookin for a big permotion, Sarge?

Mind your cheek, young fella, and take note of who you're addressin.

Yea an you watch who you're accusin.

So you refuse to own up and admit to your own involvement, even when your friend Goat has pointed the finger at you?

Even if that's true what good will it do me to admit it? If I'm goin to be hung it might as well be for a sheep. You're barkin up the wrong tree, Mister Sarghint, I say. I'll not admit to some'hin I didn't do nor know nothin about.

He continue to threaten me, an this arguin go round an round in circles til in the end the auld bollix gets up an walks out. I'm left there stewin in me own juices for ages, til he finally come in to me again. Get up outa that an don't ever have me callin for you any more, you hear?

Blessed is the innocent for they shall see the kingdom of Heaven, I says, takin a line from the sermon the cuinnic give the evenin before.

Get outa here ya thievin little tinker, auld Grunter hisses.

Remember Our Lord's message, I remind him again, an he make a run at me.

Straight away I compare notes wuth Goat.

It turn out Grunter never go near him.

*

A week later Noddy chair another meetin of the Pavee Club. Last time we do a job on the black widda, he begins, and our new member here get the third degree for his troubles from Muog Gillick, but he show great spirit standin up to the bully. I'm in no doubt who you'd like to get your own back on this time, Whacker.

I give him a nod.

Sorry pal, but it's Stacie's turn this time, ain't it Goat?

She's the main cause of me nightmares.

Next they have a argument. I make it me business to stay out of it. A run-in wuth the sarghint's plenty for one week.

What kinda prank ye want to pull? Noddy aks.

Poison her cats, Goat say.

Then the cats would suffer. How about pourin weedkiller on her lawn, or pullin up her shrubs?

Poison her thoroughbreds!

Jesus, you're at it again! Ya want to poison every'hin belongin tiv her. There's a vicious streak in you, Hussey.

Bred up in me from me father an mother, Nod.

There's some'hin twisted bout you.

No way, Stokes. I no different from anyone else far as I know.

Well you is. Quit this shit about harmin animals.

How bout puttin sugar in her petrol tank? I says.

That's more like it.

Or slash the auld cow's tyres?

Spot on, Whack, says Nod.

Or burnin her car some night wuth petrol? Goat say again.

Would that not be goin a bit too far now?

Ye say she breeds thoroughbreds? I aks.

So? says Nod.

Why not slip an auld mongrel in with her prize bitch some night just after she come intiv heat?

Not only that but you'd want to slip him in just fore she takes her to Slattery's to be serviced, says Noddy.

Looks like you've given it some thought already, Goat says to me.

Jesus pals, Noddy complain. This is gettin fierce complicated. Too many things can go wrong here an fore you know it we could be up shit creek. Play some'hin simple.

But look at the surprise she'll have when she go out to the shed an sees these ugly-lookin yokes that's supposin to be prize setters? Wouldn't that be a mighty prank?

The other two is a kinda comin round tiv me way a thinkin.

Lettin an auld mongrel into her shed – wouldn't that create a cruel fierce ruction? Goat say.

Sure isn't they always barkin? Isn't the people all the day an night complainin? Some nights they's so loud they'd wake the dead! Only she's that well got wuth Gillick she a been persecuted ages ago, says Noddy.

But how is you to know the rale right time to plant the mongrel? Goat aks.

Well, I know Slattery from comin intiv the hotel. I could cuter it out of him wuth a bit a coaxin. I'll tell him I know someone who's anxious to get one of her pups, an when will she be comin into season again? I might hit it lucky with him. If I do I'll get back to ye.

I sees two more problems, says Goat.

Well spit them out, Noddy say.

Put a cur in with her prize bitch for the night. When she come out in the mornin she'll spot him.

Let him out fore mornin, I says.

That solve that. What's the other?

What'll happen to them ugly-lookin pups?

She won't be able to sell them that's for sure.

You know what she'll do then?

Nod say nothin, but I can guess.

They'll drown them in the river that's what.

So? Noddy say.

Isn't that cruelty to dogs? What's the differ between that an poisonin her prize bitch?

How can you tell what she's goin to do wuth the pups? Beside this prank's a great challenge, isn't it Whack?

Tis be Jesus.

That's settled. I'll tell you what, Goat. You want to slash

them tyres or put sugar in her tank, then go right ahead. Be our guest.

We break up on that note.

Two day later I get a nod from Goat. As luck would have it she's already in season. Slattery tauld her she's to bring her dog tiv him tomorrow, so we must act quick. We agree to doin it this way. Goat bring Eyebrows to the shed that evenin an I'll creep up there at dawn an let him out.

A few day later I meet Nod in the street. The job went well, I hear.

Not a hitch in the big wide world.

Browser enjoyed himself?

He have a grin on him from ear to ear an I lettin him out.

Let nature take her course then.

# 5

When you not brought up in a cean, Pecker, it's hard to live in one. At furst we have plenty a space but no furniture or carpets. Instead, we use wooden crates for chairs an we have one table for the kitchen. Me granny prefer a tilly lamp cause when you turn on the light bulb the dirt ushta jump up at you an put her to shame. The rest of hus don't give a shite, but the grand queen rule the roost in these things.

Outside the trees be wide awake, pinin in the wind for me to return tiv the wild. How can one stand to stay rooted in the one spot without movin, the main notion runnin through me da's head as well, an we both lookin at the scenery thro' the same auld stupid windie.

Like wild animals in a cage – I'm more like a rat in a box. Twould drive a man ruilla, this auld cean, father complain, grittin his teeth an bangin on the wall, an I knowin his tongue's hangin out for a lush of the traipe.

Upstairs is a place everyone dread. Better left tiv the bats an barn owls, me da say. I mane how can anybody in his right mind shleep an he lyin a mile off the ground? – an everyone agreein wuth him.

I try it a few times but it ushed to give me a lightness too. You no sooner close your eyes an you feel like swirlin. It ushed to bate me how the townies an buffers be able for it. Suppose it have to do wuth the way they's brought up.

So we all sleep on the hard flure downstairs. Me granny thrun her mattress out. That yoke's too soft for a pavee, she growl.

The big problem bout movin is decidin what to bring. In the end no one want to throw out any'hin, so we use the upstairs for to store all kinds a things like waxy, rags, lanterns, lead, coney skins, halters, jam jars – two pound an one pound sizes – porter dreepers – pints an half pints – copper, brass an tin, horse hair mixed wuth donkey's – pure junk of all kinds. Scavengers we is, Pecker. Any'hin that glitter we collect like jackdaws.

*

When I look at the photos an I see me mother in them she has lovely thick jet black hair partin even on both sides from the tip of her forehead, turnin her face intiv a white egg shape. Oh how I ushed to long to hug her wuth those smilin eyes of hers, the brows thick black too an dimples – they gets turned intiv wrinkles later – an a grin you couldn't help but admire wuth pearly white teeth glistenin from the scrubs wuth the black ash from a burnt stick. Some people is just born beautiful.

An how can I describe the granny of the cean – the auld queen herself the hair on her head as thick an long as me mother's but gone grey an straggly like the grain in an ash split be lightnin, an wuth no teeth left it turn her jowls all wrinkly like ripply water, an her eyes gone all sad an watery too, her body ailin.

At no time would she be without her black shawl hangin on be a thread tiv her slim curvin shoulders an her white blouse wuth dugs gone withered inside an her legs goin wobblin in her black leather boots.

Jesus, how they ushed to go stampin round tiv the rhythm of a jiggy tune of a concertina on a footpath in the main street of Killorglin for the Puck Fair years ago. Those be the days, she keen be the glimmer, after a feed a flowery cullions an sendin up great puffs a smoke outa her dudgeen.

Me auld bones isn't able for the tober anymore, she sigh fore droppin off for a nap, which would drive the auld man mad cause it's her an me ma an their relations that has him trapped in the helm. No feckin woman's goin ta clip me wings, he complain when he lose his temper.

Nor has he given up on his dream neither. He still have his caravan parked out in the back yard much tiv the annoyance of our neighbours, but that's nothin compared tiv the ruilla builla he caused later wuth all the scrap piled up in the front garden.

One evenin he's a visit from the shadogs, pullin up outside our cean in their black squad car, an Pork Chops an Sargint Gillick wuth the muog's head. Jesus, there's no doubt they hate the livin sight of husses. Me da never forgive him for the corripin he get one time in the barracks fore they send him to prison.

I'm issuin you with a summons over that scrap, Gillick say. Move it, or you know what'll happen again. Remember your last visit to our own little black hole of Calcutta, Joyce? Well it'll be worse next time. Your stint in jail twill be in the 'Joy – not that holiday camp you were in last time in Marboro!

Me da promise them he'll move it, but sure enough he never do. He only sayin this to keep them off his back, cause he be a fierce stubborn man. No wonder he's all for the campin still, especially wuth all this rabusin goin on. No way is he on for throwin out the campin things – the riggin pole an wattles, the canvas cover, the whole shaggin gear he keep stored away in his precious horse-drawn caravan.

*

Travellers loves plinty a colours an when the women move intiv the cean they put on lovely flowery wallpaper in all the rooms. They hang a sacred heart lamp on the landin an anytime you look up He's starin down at ya with them funny probin eyes – remindin me all the time of the seven deadly sacraments, as me da ushed to call them, an he in one of his moods for slaggin me granny.

Me granny has some lovely framed picturs of horses, an a few others of gorgeous scenery an they's hung up too. Me mother have two great big picturs – one of Our Lord and the other of The Blessed Virgin, God resht them both, an herself an the granny puts statues in the windies like Saint Hantony, Saint Christopher, ones like that.

An then the photos of the auld people, God resht them too. The Travellers believes they should never be seen hangin in a cean. Father say they should always be hid away by theirselfs – that he's his own life to live an doesn't want to be reminded all the time about the other side cause he'll be over there soon enough himself.

Put up picturs, he say, like the childer's ones – say their Holy Communion or Confirmation, or our own weddin photos even.

Jesus, not the weddin ones, me ma complain. They remind me a purgatory. She be more than a match for him with her tongue, Pecker.

When me an your da get marrit there be no churchin ceremony at all, to say nothin about them photos, me granny say then.

Then how would you know ye got marrit if you didn't go thro' the priesht?

Sure we jumped the budget, didn't we, Cait?

Aye, that's what ye done, she say wuth a straight face, knowin full well they've me baffled. An yer late grandfather he put a ring on yer granny's finger out of a barney brack.

What's a budget? I aks.

It's nothin more than a ordinary toolbox, son.

Ya mane like d'auld toolbox in the wagon?

Auld traditions is always the best, me granny say.

For Jesus' sake what kind a ceremony's that?

That's the way she be done in the auld days, lad.

\*

Me granny she ushta love any'hin that have the shine a silver – shiny saucepints, chrome basins, any'hin that glitter, say copper or brass yokes, the auld jackdaw would take a shine to. The windies be packed wuth glass bowls an vases all full of paper flowers that's all range a colours.

Then one day they go mad on lace altogether. Me ma an the granny they spend ages puttin it on cushions an on the bedspreads even.

About the only good thing bout the cean is we ushed to have almighty dinners in the kitchen. Mother wuth a flowery apron on she lift the big silvery saucepint off the range full a those hot steamin cullions in their pale yalla jackets. British Queens me da get off this auld farmer, an she slaps it down on the bare boards of the table shoutin – Lush your gricheir to hus starvin savages – an there's hands flyin in from all directions grabbin them on tiv their plates, for there can never be a proper dinner without potatoes, them an pucks a cob, an a few roomogs or a lock a carnish from the grunter – tome peck for a pavee feen, an you wash it all down wuth mugs a fountie, Pecker.

Father sayin, I'll need creels on this plate ta hauld the chuck. Jesus, you swear I'd worms. I so hungry I could ate a scabby babby – scabs furst. Go aisy aan the grunter there, Whack!

How bout a pig trough? I say, cause I can be as thick as the best.

Shut up ya stoomer or I'll give ya a belt of the back a me hand.

He's a savage at the table but a chicken at the work, me granny say.

That don't go down too well.

Bring me a bull, me da say then. Cut his horns off an wipe his arse an I'll ate him no bother. Mevvy I leave ya the tail, he say tiv me gran, for to make ya some soup.

I taste a bit a heaven an a mighty lock a hell in me life, says me gran, but I'll take hell anatime.

I'd prefer a bull in me oven, says me ma, which make me father splurt his peck all over the table wuth a blast a laughter.

Later liftin a slice a turnover loaf to his mouth, he laugh when the joke occur again tiv him an it fall outa his hand. How come they always hits the floor butter side down? he complain. Liftin it up he take a gawk at all the matted hairs along wuth how's your father else be stuck on it fore stickin it inta Eyebrowser's eager gob.

No wonder dogs doesn't live long, he say then.

Eyebrowser lap up the dirty slice in five seconds flat.

Later me mother go intiv the bedroom for to breast-feed the babby.

Don't be givin Mulchas all that mate without a potato, me da sneer after her.

Wuth a pair like hers no one need ever go hungry in this cean, me gran give me a wink.

43

We wouldn't want to be dependin on yours, me da grunt.

*

The queen a the cean in her black shawl an dress, her belly full at long last, sit back in her own special chair after gettin me to put a heap a trimmers on the glimmer an tho' twouldn't be cold, her blood's thin. There's a fierce lot said to be warm. Isn't it true, Whack? she say, an out with her dudgeen again an she send up great rings a smoke fit to purr like a cat, she love her peck.

Then she start talkin about her favourite foods. One of the nicest things, Whack, is goose soup. Ya bile up yer goose in a big pot wuth plinty a water, chopped onion, potato an turmicks, an plinty a salt thrun in, an whin he's done, all ya do is dish out a cup a soup each to every member of the family. Oh Jesus, there's nothin finer than a good slug a goose soup.

Wuth a mouth like hers she'd need a bucketload. Me da give me a nip. Yuk, he say then, makin a face. I'm glad ya never try that on hus. More sharper than castor oil, I'd swear.

Divil the scutters you'll get. Sure we's bred up tiv eatin an drinkin all kinds a greasy tack.

Jesus, Whack, that one musht have the stomach of a horse.

Roashted hedgehog in a milk sauce wuth hawthorn buds, that's the loveliest feed I ever ate in me whole life, she say tiv me then.

Me auld man on hearin that clear out the dure.

Yuk, I says, fit to vomit at the thought.

Oh Jesus no, Whack. His taste is a cross between a grunter an a creeper.

Don't tell me ya ate a cat too?

Jusht like a chicken, she grin, smackin her lips.

That be me grandmother. You never know when she be pullin your leg.

Wance upon a time I be told this, son, she say then, by a forkin teller. There's such a curse on this auld country that even the richest in it is never more than a week away from the famine an the poorest no more than a day. So keep that in mind, lad. Enjoy your peck as you find it. That's me advice tiv you now. Live life to the full, cause the day will come soon enough when you'll run out of a thing they call time.

# 6

Any'hin like the rows an rabusin that go on in the cean be only unnatural. Father he's nearly like a worse weasel without the drink than wuth it. Pinin for the open road, especially if the weather's good.

Sittin there wuth a face on him like two pissholes in the snow. What a grand mild night to be out in, he's frettin.

The moon shaded by misty cloud shiftin to a lovely soft breeze you can walk in without your jacket on, an creepers slinkin about pouncin at a shiftin leaf or twitchin snout. Jesus Christ Almighty, what am I doin cooped up in here, an that grand mad moon above hus? he complain.

I'm agreein wuth him, while I gaze across at the Slieve Blooms shrouded in a driftin fog, makin them look more like ghosts instead of the real thing.

I knows only too well how he feel. Me mind shoot back tiv that magic time when I'm about six, lyin on me back on the floor of the cart and a night jusht like this one, me da hunched up front hauldin the reins in the clear black an blue night glimmerin wuth stars.

Did ya ever notice how quiet the stars is? he say tiv me.

But that evenin me mind's on other things. Jesus, I'd love ta be rich like them Cashes, I says.

What need have you for grade on a glorious night like this,

46

lad, wuth the moon above for a pearl beyant price an the stars for your diamonds? Isn't there great wealth up there that we all can share?

But how can ya pick them? I aks. Where could ya sell them?

You has the makins of a rale flash pavee, son, me da laugh.

Of course I know how much he's in his element when out on the road.

Sittin about wuth nothin to do that's what ushta annoy me da an me the most. I'd get up an leave an go out an see Goat. His father, the Puckeen Hussey, our next door neighbour an me uncle, he some solid block of a man in them days, built like a tank, an a mighty yoke to brag. As a bare-knuckle boxer he's tome, wuth no one round to beat him. Still his fists is more than a fair match for his mouth.

When it come to babby-makin tho', he's tame enough, for barrin Goat's Tail all of his childer is girdles, an like himself the whole lot of them have red hair, God bless the mark.

Aside from the boxin he's also a great man to work. You see him up on the trailer there grabbin polytin bags a turf off of hus, an standin them up on the floor. One of them fall an he prop him up again. Stand up outa that, ya gomey auld fucker, he shout, when he see him topplin over again. Jesus, if ya was human I'd knock ya flat wuth a belt. Hurry on up outa that the lock of ye with them bags. Yis is like a bunch a cows of a wet day wadin in muck an shite round fodder! That's the sort a man he be, Pecker – an the reason so few want to take him on in a fight.

Two things about the Husseys. Like hus, they love to keep animals in their cean, an the other thing they isn't afraid to sleep upstairs. The Puckeen have creepers galore along wuth a sight a dogs. If a pup's not the full shillin at birth, he have no hesitation drownin him in the river.

He's some hoor of a get when it come to breedin.

One other thing they have in common wuth hus – their house is as big a mess as ours. One room downstairs, the Puckeen have a litter of foxhounds livin in it, an a tome man too to rear them. Sure the farmers come from far an wide for his pups.

Go tell that auld lad a yours he's a lazy good for nothin, the Puckeen shouts at me this day an I visitin Goat. Of course he's only half-slaggin. Still, there's a message in it. That's what me da don't like about him. He's far too gruff for his taste.

Arra, leave the lad alone, his thin frail little wife say. Sure it's not his fault.

While she's sayin that, I'm rememberin the four things me da says the Husseys is noted for – sharp tongues, red hair, fightin an thievin.

Unlike me father, the Puckeen's cute enough an well able to look after himself. The drink – an be Jesus he love gallons of it – never seem to knock him off his stride, while it dog me own auld da. He'll be up at cockcrow an gone all day about his business – scrap mostly, an a bit of smugglin me father tell me on the q-t. There's no flies on the Puckeen Hussey, I can tell you.

One day a short time later the Puckeen comes flyin in our door. Blocker, he says, I know where there's a mighty job.

Unfortunately he catch him in a foul mood.

If the job be anyways middlin at all ya woulda grabbed it for yourself, he grunts back.

What's botherin you now, boy? the Puckeen cries. Lyin back there idle as a piper's little finger. Is d'auld skyhope gettin ya nervy agin, eh?

Anyways, after a day or two me da take heed tiv his brother-in-law an sets out to work for a farmer in the country, a quare buffer in his fifties be the name a Matty Madden, wuth drooped shaulders an a huge pot belly bulgin out, an a great big thick red head on him, who wouldn't find the winter stealin over him he's that lazy. All the donkey work goin, that's what father get, like cleanin out cowhouses, liftin smelly shit intiv a big wheelbarrow wuth the graipe, an he often bring me to wheel it wobblin over tiv the big dung heap.

Then we go cut turf wuth the slean for the auld fella. Again he call on me for to wheel the barrow out onto the cutaway for spreadin, an tough goin she is too.

That evenin the two of hus comes back tiv his house, bandy-legged an goggly-eyed wuth exhaustion, an auld Creeper Madden remarks to me poor auld da in the yard, his cunnin oglers blinkin – There'll be no barney tonight, Blocker Joyce – which I don't rightly understand then.

But it make him mutter the minute Creeper turn to go inside to fetch hus the money for the day, There's no way you'd want ta get below the bottom board in that auld geezer. Dig too deep there, son, an God knows what kinda dirt ya might find.

An on the way home after payin hus a lousy few deener for breakin our arses, I says, Suppose he's too mane for ta get marrit, daddy?

But he keep his mouth shut.

He's too old now?

Too quare in his ways, me da mumble.

Let him go ate the thick end of a shite for himself then, I say, actin cocky an feelin the pain of the welts that ruz on me palms from the day's wheelin.

He'd tip cats thro' a skylight, that fella. I is not full knowin what he mean, but guessin it probably have some'hin to do wuth that big three-letter word beginnin wuth S.

Other days we be out weedin his turmics.

It isn't long fore you feel it down along the backs of your legs I can tell ya, Pecker. All that bendin – pluckin up hundrets a millions of weeds – tryin to take over, an they'd a won too be a long shot if the turmics war dependin on Creeper Madden.

No one else would work for d'auld bollix on this kinda money, me da's all the time mutterin under his breath, or, There's got to be aisier ways of earnin a few deener, lad, but I know he's doin it for to save up an buy a few tome curras.

Other days he have you out savin hay or footin turf, then drawin it an heapin it in the shed. Jesus there's no end tiv the slavin, me da complain. Still so long as we's gettin the mideogs, Whack, isn't that the main item?

In the evenins he's too tired to spend it in the gat cean, so as far as the family's concerned things is lookin up in a manner of speakin.

*

Any'hin like the rows that be ruz in our cean, Pecker, an they'd rise outa nothin. Me mother's callin me Jack or John an the da start slaggin me.

Whack's yer monicker, lad, an don't you mind them snazzy-wazzy airs of yer mother. Sure she's a Hussey an can't help it.

An we has good reason too, me ma say. Sure me great ancestors be kings an queens of Ireland wance, til them Limeys comes over an take our land, an we all get turfed out on the tober an we been travellin ever since.

Arra don't be mindin her, Whack. She's only bullin ya wuth fairy tales her family make up, especially yer granny. Sure Puckeen's the vera same next dure. Just cause he's big intiv bare

50

knuckle boxin that qualify him ta be King a the Tinkers, eh? What's that got to do wuth pedigree?

Well the cream always come tiv the top, me ma say. An consider yerself lucky you marrit into some.

Yis, an you go down to Flynn's shop to fetch some milk, an d'auld queen there isn't long puttin ya in yer place. Kings an queens me arse. Let's face it, we's nothin but trash in their eyes. An me da go into a big long sulk. Then he say, On the road or round the molly, thems the only places we can be free. In the cean you must pay the rint an a million other bills. Ya can't piss aan yer own front lawn without the whole town complainin, an you has people lookin in an seein what yer havin for breakfast, or whether yer goin ta Mass, or how yer keepin the backyard. Have ya got a licence for yer van? Me dogs is supposed to be dummies.

Well if that's how you is feelin, why don't you go back on the road an give hus a bit a peace? me mother complain.

Ya know that's just what I might go an do, he sneers back at her.

# 7

I think me da's only coddin her, but later inta the summer, when he have a fair bit a deener saved workin for Madden, he rig up the auld horse-drawn caravan an take me wuth him down to the Puck Fair in Killorglin in the County Kerry where there's a great gatherin a Travellers, an me da know a fierce lot of them.

The tarred road's a fierce an lively yoke on a curra, his hooves glancin off its hard sliddery surface betimes near tumblin him til he get used tiv it.

God be wuth the days fore the paved roads, son, he say tiv me then. Nowadays the birds – they don't know theirselfs.

What you mean? I aks.

The gravelled roads. Sure we ushta meider them wuth stones outa the hand or pebbles outa slings an catapults – sharp-shootin them in trees, on walls or in hedges, son.

An is that the way for a pagan to behave?

If you want to survive a famine, boy, you may eat any'hin that move bar grass.

Next day, he return wuth a sack that have some'hin movin in it.

Son, he say, foosterin wuth his hand inside, we is goin ta make a sight a garaid this week wuth this fella.

He pull a lovely-lookin snow white duck outa the bag.

We'll set up our own little stall in this field, alongside the rest, an sure tiv be Jesus we'll make a mighty skullin. By week's end this duck he be worth his weight in gold yet, you mark them words.

I can't make head nor tail of this. How ya goin ta make money outa one auld duck, dad?

Be getting him ta dance.

Is he trained?

There's no need.

What make you so sure he goin to do the job?

I intend leavin him wuth no other choice.

So he sets up his little stall in the field, alongside a long line of them sellin any'hin you care to mention from brass an leather things to pottery, glass ornaments, paper flowers, tin buckets or to even tellin your forkin.

What he do is a kinda cruel. He get himself a sheet of galvanized an puts a little gas stove under it, an gets me to collect the money in his peaked cap from the crowd gathered round. An be Jesus is there not some fierce gang of our own. Some can't believe what they's seein. You stand on a hot plate in your bare feet, Pecker, an you'll dance a mighty tune fierce well too. Wouldn't ya?

The crowd knock great gallery outa this dancin duck, an leave behind a powerful lock a mideogs.

Now, son, me da say after we count the takings that evenin, The rale tough time for me is jusht about ta begin. All me pals is around an if I start drinkin, I won't last the week. So I've made a plan, an I want you ta follow out yer end. No matter how hard I plead wuth ya durin the night, turn a deaf ear, ya hear?

Whatever ya say, boss.

That night an he lyin down, he gets me to lock a dog chain round his legs an fasten it round a spring under the caravan wuth a clasp. He sleeps like a log that night, but the followin evenin he begin to wail some'hin fierce, beggin me for to open the lock. His tongue's stickin out for a jar, an I give him a sup a lemonade instead, but that only seem to make him worse.

There's vinegar on the shelf yonder. Give me a sup a that.

Jesus, but that only make you sick, da.

They say it made outa wine.

Yea, but there's no kick tiv it.

How you know?

Cause you tell me that yourself onetime.

Next night I get vera little sleep. I keep him at his word. I refuse to go near the key.

By the end of the second day the duck's feet gets so sore me da have to go buy another couple a drakes, but toward the end of the week he make a sight a deener.

Good for ya, I says.

We'll buy a few foals now, he say. This the time to buy them at the right price, for the daylers be too greedy at the beginnin of the week. They start to panic now an let them off right.

\*

Me da he ushta love to dayle a lot in animals in his time, Pecker – donkeys, but mostly horses he'd buy in fairs like Puck, Cahirmee, Spancil Hill or Ballinasloe, an drive them easht an sell them at a fancy profit.

He ushta buy them cheap from small farmers too in the west. A blocker is what they ushta call a man like that in them days – Blocker Joyce – an Jesus he show me mighty ways a daylin, like stickin a ball a ginger or a dab a pepper up the auld nag's arse to make her prance good an lively like. I remember him do that one time to a pony at the fair in Bartlemee an he sold him in a flash. We is many miles down the tober fore the farmer be any the wiser.

Or he'd file an auld knacker's teeth to make her look younger. One time visitin a farm a fine colt catch his eye. That night he steal back an feed him some chaff. Next day he return back to buy the horse. He's coughin an chokin so bad the farmer sell him for a song.

But tell me, da, I says, Is that not a sin what you do there?

Not at all, Whack. Isn't we getting one up on the buffers?

But Missus Crowley in the national school say we can beg but on no account is we to rob off our neighbours.

The Ten Commandments she be talkin about, eh?

Yis, da. They's supposed to be followed.

Only if yer settled.

An is we not settled?

You might be, but I isn't.

Well I never heard the beatin of it, Pecker. You learn some'hin new every day, I says tiv me da.

At your age stick wuth the moochin, ya hear? he say then. Yer too young ta go trickin yet. Mevvy whin yer finished school.

Jesus, me mouth drop an he mentionin that horrid kip. I is under the impression I'm too auld an can leave all that behind me now that we's moved intiv the town. You say school? I aks.

One of the joys a livin in the helm. Yer still fourteen, son, an I guarantee the sarge be on tiv you come September. You wait an see. Any'hin to make life difficult for hus, Gillick be on the mark.

Mevvy I'll go for a week.

Look I know this schoolin's only a cod for the mosht part. As I say tiv ya earlier, the few sums an a bit a readin an writin is OK, but too much edificatin knock the cleverness outiv ya.

We go over to gawk at a few more mares an foals, an he start learnin me bout the horses to avoid.

Suddenly he turn to face me. I learn me lessons the hard way, son – in the school of hard knocks. Whin I war round yer own age, me father sint me on me own tiv the fair ta sell a fine staub of an ass, an before I'm any the wiser this crowd a pavees gets me mad drunk in the gat cean, an then this rale shmart fella he slip a few quid in me pocket. Then he say, Time I got goin or I'll never get yer donkey home.

What donkey? I says, me mouth droppin.

Sure the wan ya jusht sold me!

Be Jaysus I never sold ya no ass.

Well I seen him put the money in your coat pocket, his mate interrupt hus then. It's in that pocket there! Am I right or wrong, Red? he aks another mate he's in cuckoots wuth in the gang.

An like a right auld drunken gomey, I put me hand in me pocket an feels the deener. I walk home fierce confused for they is after goin an doin a swingle aan me.

He stop an stares intiv me eyes, his face gone all twisted an serious. See that dead lurog in me head, son? he say rale nervous, an he takin a look round him to see if anyone's comin. Seein the coast is clear, he whisper, The night I bring home the few deener for the donkey, me auld lad he take off his leather belt an corrip'd the lard outa me round the molly. Next thing doesn't the pin outa the brass buckle get caught in me eye. There's blood gushin, an in the blind pain the ogler wint dead. No use to me ever again. I can tell ya it done me head in in

56

more ways than one. It put me rightly aan the traipe, I can assure ya, Whack.

His story have me own head spinnin I can tell you. It haunt me tiv this very day, an explain a fierce lot about me da.

He take me on a walk round the field where the ponies an horses is. You notice I never hit ya in yer life, Whack, tho' God knows I come close tiv it many the time, but after the larrupin I get I swore I'd never raise a hand tiv any of me own. Come aan, I see a nice lock a foals over here an listen tiv me do the daylin. That way you'll learn a lot more than you ever will in all them schools.

By the final Sunday he's a rake of them bought an he's still on the dry, so we set off for home, travellin up thro' Tipperary where the farmers goes mad for his ponies, an he coulda sell ten time the amount an make fierce money. The hardest job's keepin a few good ones for himself. Me da be a mighty man to trade in horses. About that there's no doubt, Pecker.

Now that he's in the mood for confessin there's one question I'm dyin to aks. I spring it on him this evenin on the way home. Auld Muog Gillick, da. Why he have it in so much for hus?

Oh that go back a long way when he's just a ordinary guard. A mate a mine get hauled in for stealin turf off the bog. I wouldn't mind but he never do it. Of course it's Grunter's style to pin it on the weak ones. Lookin for a promotion – he get one too in the end.

Anyway I follows them back tiv the barracks an hide behind a shrub that's growin near the windie an that way I'm able to peep in. Any'hin like the corripin me mate get that afternoon – well Gillick he bate the livin daylights outa him. He write out a statement for him to sign. Then handin the fella the pen, he grab his hand an write his signature for him on the paper.

It have him admittin to stealin the turf while every dog in the street know Con Guiney, the sheep shagger, take it. After that he slap him in the cell. Next thing he get called out. He lep on his bike an away up the road wuth him.

I sneak in, lift the key off the nail on the wall an let out me mate, but Jesus an we leavin doesn't Grunter's young son catch sight of me. Me mate skip it off to England an haven't been seen since. The young lad give the shadogs me description. In time I gets hauled in.

There's no way I'm goin to confess to some'hin I didn't do, I keep tellin them. You can go check it if ye want but yesterday evenin I be with me brother twenty mile away, so how can I be here? You is barkin up the wrong tree, Guard Gillick, I say.

Next thing they bring in the young fella. Yes, he say, that's him.

How is I to know ye didn't put him up to sayin that? You is goin to take the word of a seven-year-old again mine?

We are, Grunter nod his thick head, cause I know he's tellin the truth.

The judge will have no bother throwin that outa court, I say.

In the end they has no choice but to let me go, an Gillick's ragin cause he know I done it, an he's hopin to pin the stealin on me mate so he can get a leg up in the world. He have it in for me ever since.

When we get home, he leave his prize ponies out in a field he rent off the Creeper Madden. I can see a look a satisfaction on his face an he leavin them. Sure they nearly make up for havin ta live in that auld cean, wuth that ruilla auld granny a yours, he say to me an he closin the gate. That night he go on a fierce mad tear wuth the deener he's left from the dancin duck. He go so hard on it durin the followin week he end up in Marboro Asylum to dry out.

# 8

After a few weeks in Saint Fintan's me da return a very tame man. It's then he begin to miss the bit a garaid we ushta make when doin the moochin.

The trouble about beggin round your own helm is that the townies don't be long gettin sick of ye, an even at the weekends when the mideogs is flush, we isn't gettin shag all a them as me da be noticin, so he'd round hus up intiv his van an drive off intiv another county.

Livin in Offaly we has seven of them borderin hus to choose from. Often we bring Goat's young sister too. Furst we make her all dirty lookin an get her to wear tattered auld rags.

The ma tell me whin I be a babby she make sure to bring me along, dirty face an all, wuth snot runnin down me nose, an that grand big nopper a golden curdles.

How could the buffers say no to givin me a few deener? Indeed, you better than the gladar box, she say. A rale money-makin machine you be in them days, Whack, an whin I'm too busy to go moochin meself, the neighbours 'id be queuein up ta borra you for to go beggin theirselfs.

The auld wicker basket's a mighty yoke too for gettin yer foot in the dure, so you fill it full wuth paper flowers, wooden clothes-pegs, tinware, shoelaces, scissors, darnin needles, spools a thread, ballad sheets, mothballs, rosary badyses, holy midals –

any'hin a buffer in a backward spot might need. I ushta find this a lot more respectable way a doin business than moochin in the street, Pecker.

One Saturday, me da's tongue stickin out for a drink, so he take me off to mooch in Tellamore. I use all the advice me family give me about beggin to great effect an I do well too, an wuth me auld man takin it accordin as I is earnin it, he's in mighty fettle on the traipe by evenin time.

When we get home, he take me intiv the gat cean wuth him for a lemonade so he can scull a few more down the hatch. It's the evenin fore the Offaly footballers is about to play Dublin in Marboro in the second round of the Leinster Championship, an there's great excitin talk goin on about the teams in the bar when we walks in.

Me da know feck all bout football. Sure who'd want to be watchin a bunch a grown men chase a bag a wind up an down a field? he'd say when aksed.

Hey, Blocker! Who's goin to win tomorrow? Bartholomew Brock call out on seein hus. Some call him Bart, others Barty, an he's some mighty great ballyragger. He own a big lump a bog out the tober an get rakes a men to work for him all durin the summer, cuttin, haypin an drawin turf. That's how me da come to know him, an Bart treat him well.

Sure what would a Galway tinker know about Offaly football? Willie Nash, this big stuck up farmer who kick wuth the other foot, shout back.

Watch what ya call me friend, Nasher! says Bart, wavin hus over. Talk about a clanny lot, Blocker. I'll bet ya if that Nash fucker look into his family tree, he'll find some rare monkeys swingin from the branches.

Bart's not afraid of insultin anyone.

This is one argument me da definitely don't want to get intiv, but Bart's well oiled an want to knock more gallery outa this banter about pedigree.

Jesus, if I was dyin of the hunger I'd ate a black puddin outa rat's blood ahead of a Nash's any day, says he clappin me da on the back. What's yer tack, Block?

Ah, the divil's buttermilk will do me lovely, thanks Barty.

An the chip off the auld Block? What'll he be havin?

Oh, a drop a red lemonade will do him fine, says me auld lad on me behalf.

Jesus, talkin about blood, Blocker, says Bart, aimin his spake again at Nash. Sure tinker blood's the purest – Joyces, Wards, McDonaghs – the finest Gaelic brand names outa the top drawer. Look at the heads in this pub – Wallace's, Turley's, Nash's there. I'd bet there's Turk's blood somewhere in that cunt. Now here's Sean O'Connor beside me. As Irish a name as you'll get. Am I right or wrong on that, Seanie?

Tis indeed, Bart, he stutters.

Still yer auld one's a Blunny, an that's far from pure! Sure yer nothin but a screwed up Paddy. Then there's that other gang a yis that come up be the Land Commission from outa the west. Ye call yerselfs Offaly min? A canny shower that used to cut the horns off their sheep so they could graze the grass between the rocks. No wonder yis jump at the chance to grab our land. An take a look at Finnerty there with an eye on him like a hungry gannet. All the way outa Roscommon where the women's scarce an the sheep nervous. Ye want a good tip on who to marry for a lock a land? Go to Finnerty, folks!

Nash is standin there pretendin to be takin this rale calm, concentratin on his pipe he is, goin thro' the motions of preparin for the smokin – packin, tappin, an packin, then lightin it rale deliberate like – the kick from the inhalin makin him look lively again.

You Nash! Stand back there fore I do-bar ya with me fist into yer monkey gob. Bart swaggers a step or two in his direction. And your side-kick beside ya there with his long narra head. Put a whiskers under his sniffer an he be a dead ringer for a rat.

His side-kick's definitely hurtin. He just stand there fruze in the one spot, his lips pursed intiv a tight O, puckered like a tom cat's arsehole when he have his bush tail up.

Jesus, Nasher, ya wouldn't hit a bull's arse wuth a banjo. If I gave ya a bale a hay to wipe yer arse, you'd still end up with shite on yer fingers.

All this banter draw an odd laugh from the crowd. Most of them work for Brock on the bog. A self-made man is Bart. Wide in the butt – stocky, but well built. There's nothin but lean mate on him, wuth huge muzzles in his shaulders, an arms as long as a chimp's, which put me to thinkin it's him they should be callin a monkey, an wuth his surname he's probably as big a blow-in as the rest he's criticisin.

Next thing he turns to the barman – Paddy, he say out for all to hear, I remember yer auld lad well. A fierce canny man too who well understood the meanin of, It's for his own good the cat purrs. Remember when yis have that pub in Tellamore?

Sure, Bart.

Yer auld fella was the only man on the main street ever to keep pigs in his own back yard. Remember that?

Kind of, he say.

Everyone in the pub is all ears now.

Anyways, you'll hardly ever go back to rearin them?

Very doubtful.

That's a pity. Bart's smirkin at Nash an his mate. Seein you have the odd few visitin ya occasionally.

Me da lets out this little grunt of a laugh. Nash is gettin red round the gills now, an a bunch a drinkers is sniggerin to theirselfs.

Anyways, before the night's over he buys me da a sight a drink, an make it his business to be favourin hus over his own gang. Bart catches one of them gawkin over at hus. Show some respect now, Feery! he shout at him through the smokey air. You're nothin but a half-caste yerself, ya little shrivelled up bollix! Doesn't that cast in yer eye prove it! Sure Scotland Yard an the FBI together, they'd stand a better chance a findin Adam an Eve's shite than solvin yer pedigree. Scully, what you starin at?

There's no law again it! I can gawk where I like.

Look away this second or I'll give ya a belt that'll land you in hell where you'll be peggin in the best of my black turf into Satan's furnaces to keep the eternal flames blazin on the rest of ye mouldy fuckers when yer all dead an gone.

Can't wait til you end up in it as well an the devil put you in charge. Sure the fire definitely die, you be that fuckin mane ta peg in yer own turf, mouths Scully.

My, isn't he the cocky fella. Ye know where he get that from? Wasn't his auld one an O'Daly – the ugliest meanest fuckin rottenst auld hag that ever inhabit the globe! How could you be any different, Scully?

Tell me, Barty. Who ya reckon will win the football tomorrow? me da aks, fierce anxious to get him from startin a ruction.

Don't mind me, he shout back. Who ya think will win yerself?

64

I know shag all bout that, says the da. I'll be out there all right sellin flags an hats an bars a chocolate an oranges an the William pears. It won't bother me who win so long as I make a lock a deener.

Come on outa that, Joyce. Show some guts. Who ya reckon will win?

Suppose twill depend on who our little friends is backin.

Little friends? What ya mane?

Ye can sneer all ye like, but I has a great regard for them. They is me very own garden angels.

I take it you're referrin to the fairies, Bart say, bein reminded of a similar chat they have before on the bog.

I is.

The minute I hear this I know the traipe's got intiv me father's head.

And you's a great believer in these little people?

Always remember, Barty, you never alone in this world, even whin ya think you's on yer own. Sure the fairies is always close by – so close they be even brushin up agin ya.

They might even be feelin ya?

Sometimes. As I say before, I sees them as me protectors.

Me father's too drunk to notice, but I see Brockser winkin at one of his cronies. Bart's fillin me da up wuth booze to knock some gallery out of him.

Well, Mister Joyce, if you is a believer in fairies, where you stand with regards to your belief in God?

I'm a tinkerin man, Barty. As I already tell ya I'm a pagan. I adore the father of hus all – the sun, an his lonely daughter Luna.

Who's that when she's at home?

She's shinin over hus this very night in all her glory.

Sure the auld moon's only a big ball a rock, Blocker.

Oh she a lot more than that. See how she can swing the tides, an make min mad?

Does that mean ya never go ta Mass?

Mevvy for a weddin or a funeral for to please me family or relations. But what would a pagan be doin goin ta Mass for?

True for ya. Bart wink across at one of his pals. Now changin the subject, Blocker. Would it be possible you might be able to get one or two of yer little fellas to give the Dublin goalie a few jostles at the right times durin the game tomorrow?

I could certainly ask.

Yer not pullin me leg now, Mister Joyce?

By God I amn't, Master Barty. There's fairies everywhere we go – left and right – fornenst an behind hus.

Be the livin Jesus, ya never said a truer word. They is everywhere all right. Just look at Nash over there. Mister Willie Wagger Nash! What ya have to say for yerself? Hey monkey puss, I'm talkin to you!

Nash must be regrettin he ever call me father a tinker, cause Bart just keep on givin him no end a stick.

The big thick buffer can't take the heat no longer neither. Lowerin his pint, he slam the glass on the counter an leave in a huff.

Yer well able to dish it out, ya dirty rotten black Orange get, but yer not man enough to take it! Bart shouts after him.

Little wonder Brock carries a crooked nose. As me granny say, It's often a man's mouth break his snout. Some insulted bloke mushta give him a mighty wallop there one time, Pecker.

She's well gone beyant closin time by this stage, an there's still a few of hus knockin about, an the barman's still pourin it out when there come this knock on the dure.

Shhhh biys, it's the guards, yer man hisses after peepin out the windie.

Sargint Gillick here! the Grunter shout. Open up this minute in the name of the law, Paddy Sheedy, or I'll ram yer dure in!

Like a dog wuth his tail between his legs, Sheedy click open the lock. The burly Gillick himself wobbles in on his hind trotters, holdin a big black torch which he slap down on the counter, the crowd of hus like mice, includin Bart which is surprisin cause he's sayin all night he's afraid a no one, but Brock don't keep quiet for long. You'll have a pint, Sarge, says he rale cocky like.

Not while I'm on duty, Mister Brock, which would be breakin the law. Besides I'm a pioneer, sir.

Next, he take out his little black book an starts writin in names. When he catch sight of hus, I can read the raw hate in them muog oglers of his.

Jeysus, Sheedy, not only are you some frigger to be servin a lad under age, but to be servin tinkers too, ya must be really hard up. Christ man, I'll be hauntin you from now on for this.

They is no different from you nor me, Sargint Gillick, Bart says. Flesh an bone just like us, don't you ever forget that – you that proudly marches up to the altar rails every Sunday for Communion. Where's yer Christian virtue now, Sargint Gillick?

Don't I go to Mass every mornin as well, which is more than that git ever done, includin yerself? the sargint spits.

You're still forgettin the Christian message. Love yer neighbour. You ever hear a that?

No need for a sermon from you this time of night, Brock. You're the one that needs talkin to. Any more of yer lip an you'll be feelin the butt end of me baton in the barracks. Your tinker friend there should be well able to tell you all about that. Wouldn't ya, Joyce? Vacate these premises immediately, or ye'll be spendin the night in the slammer.

Outside the moon's beamin above hus, like that bleached skull I stumble across, starin up at me out of the black earth in an auld Protestant graveyard one time over in some quare end a Westmeath.

The nerve of that fucker in there, Bart's hissin. That Wickla hoor have it in for all your crowd, Block. Not only that, he hate the Offaly footballers as well. There ought to be some kind a law again that kind of insultin against youse.

Ah, we's ushed tiv that, isn't we, Whack? Sure sticks an stones may hurt yer bones. Isn't that some load a shite?

Anyway, Block, if I don't see you at the match tomorrow, I'll see ya in court. Tell yer fairies to knock lumps outa that Dublin goalie, ya hear?

No better man, Barty.

Add a little prayer, Block, that they take that Wickla hoor on a long journey up the Slieve Blooms an drop him in a bog-hole.

# 9

That game in Marboro next day is a humdinger. Seein that I be born in the Tellamore spike, I consider meself a Offaly fan an this event it take on a huge importance for me. I sell outa flags an crepe hats in no time. The navy sky-blue ones goes in a shot too from the flood a fans that comes off the trains at the station.

In the meantime the auld man's workin a blue streak sellin bars a chocolate, apples, pears, Slainte orange an lemonade off his stall just inside the main gate intiv the grounds, while Ribleen's busy keepin him stocked wuth boxes an crates from the van outside an stackin them on the table for him. The little stadium's packed to captivity an me da's tongue's sharp as ever.

This Jackeen fella come over to hus in a fierce way. Where's the urinal, mister? he aks an he goin blue in the face.

I'm so skittery after last night's pints I could do wuth a arsenal meself, say me da. Over there, boss.

As for the fairies, I'd say he have a word wuth that brigade all right, for the Faithful County put in three goals past the Dublin goalie that afternoon, while up the other end, Egan, Hughes an McCormack done more than just do the business.

Jesus, what a tome day. Me pockets is bulgin wuth mideogs. Me an Goat gets separated for a while in the crowd, swirlin out the gates – the Dublin fans swarmin like a disturbed hive a bees – an they'd give you a nasty sting too – an the Leix crowd is intiv wearin blue colours as well, so we isn't expectin a robustical welcome from them neither for Offaly's famous feat.

Bejaysus, let's get outa here quick, say me da, fore them Dublin hoors rob the dead eye outa me head, an we all climb inta the van an get well out on the bog road headin toward Mountmellick, fore me Goat an Ribleen begins to feel like part of the tribe again. Blocker's a different kettle a fish. Galway born an bred – he don't mind so much who win long as he make plinty a money.

We join a huge line a cars hootin horns wuth flags an streamers flyin outa the windies. There's great ruilla builla. Sure it's not every year a shower a bogmen bates the divil out of that shower a Jackeen hoors outa the Big Smoke, Pecker.

Jesus, Greene's some boyo, an Foran feedin him, an Brereton, Cullen, Carey, an I'm only mentionin a few, Bart is goin on in the Offaly Inn, his heart flat out pumpin. An where would anyone be goin comin intiv the likes a McCormack. Red in the gills he is wuth excitement. Next tiv him is this thin, pale-lookin mot he's picked up wuth blond hair an sunken eyes, nursin a glass that have surely some'hin stronger in it than water, that's to be sure.

Good auld Blocker! he shout out tiv me father an we squeezin in the dure. The Fairy Man himself! We is on a winnin roll. Jesus, Block, yer little ones done the trick today. Who ever would imagine three goals? Jesus, is there any chance that woman next dure to you would forecast the next match, an we'd win a fortune!

Blocker stands there weighin up the prospect. More beer flowin. Cuter up that Brock fella an he might get another mighty night outa this, while me, Goat an poor little Ribleen's standin waitin getting squeezed an pushed. I don't mind too much cause I likes sizin up a crowd an listenin, but me sister, she's still weak from a dose of the flu, an the auld man about to lose his head again. I give him a nudge. We bringin Ribleen home, da.

He look relieved. Tell yer mother I be back in a short while.

The short while take over five hours. Him an Brockser come in round one in the mornin, ossified. His mot he musta leave behind or tell her to get lost or mevvy she go home wuth someone else I dunno.

I want her to tell me the Offaly team's fortune, Brock's insistin. Whatever me father's pumped intiv him, Bart want action on this matter right away. I'm guessin it have to be the Puckeen's missus for she's noted for the forkin-tellin. She have a crystal ball an all, but whether she be in the mood for it or not, now that's a different matter entirely, Pecker.

Then there's the Puckeen himself. God know what kinda mood he be in. Mevvy we see them knuckles of his blanchin, itchin for a go, mevvy at Bart's thick lantern jaw. You just wouldn't know how things be shapin up at this awkward time a night.

As it turn out, the Puckeen's fired up himself on pavee juice – homemade, an clear as maiden honey from a still outa the far end a North Mayo.

How ya, Puck? Bart slurs. Is yer missus round? Now, don't be gettin me wrong. It have nothin to do wuth a jaunt.

I think Puck might take the head off him for that remark, but he just laugh. Jesus I need her bad, says Bart. Take me outa me misery now this very minute, or I'll surely suffer a heart attack. I need to know where me fortune lie with regards to the future of this Offaly football team.

She's in bed, the Puck say quietly. A Kerry buck himself if

you was to scratch deep enough. Sure the green an yalla's a close neighbour of the tricolour any day, says he, not a bit put out, even tho' there's dogs growlin an barkin from all directions.

The neighbours be kickin up some stink next mornin, I'm reckonin. D'auld sarge be addin that on tiv the summonses he dish out already.

I'll pay her a mighty sum if she can forecast the future of this Offaly team, says Bart. What you say ta twenty pound? For better or worse. Shite or burst, as they say in Pontoon. Good news or bad, I'll take me chance. I just need to be taken out of me misery, Puck. You'll get her for me? Please!

Brockser's definitely outa his head, but Puck's eyes is widenin at the sight of the big blue note wavin in his hand. Wait a minute now, he says, an he creep up the stairs. His little sparrow is wide awake in bed. Sure a mouse shufflin outside would keep that bag a nerves awake. Puck tell her she'll be twenty pound the richer if she can tell Brockser any'hin about this famous Offaly football team. Whatever ya do, don't tell him Kerry's goin ta bate them – he tell hus afterward what he say to her.

Eventually she appear in the kitchen, wizened hair on her like a thistle gone to seed. The lines a hardship you can read all over her face. But she's genuine when it come to readin yer forkin tho'. People flock to see her from far an near. She definitely have the extra sense all right. She foretell many's a forkin or misforkin, an whatever way she have wuth that crystal ball, she's not shy bout knowledgin the people on what she see in it.

You want to know how Offaly's goin ta do in their next match? she aks Bart.

Now yer cookin wuth gas. Up front, Missus, I'm not shy

wuth the money. Twenty pound ta you – win, lose or draw. I want yer forecast.

Whack, go out next dure an get your tilly lamp, she say tiv me. This light's too bright.

I do what I'm told, an when I come back she already have the crystal ball on the table. The lectric light's turned off, an the lamp light glowin tosses quare shadows of hus all upon the walls, creatin just the right shade for them spooky spirits.

The Puckeen's missus sit like she's fruze, starin cruel hard in concentratin, the white glare of the lamp makin you think there's a mask hung on her face. There isn't a word or a sound. Even the dogs show respect by keepin still – a sure sign they feel a presence or some'hin. She scrunches her lurogs. I see some'hin vague. Green white an yalla jersies – yis, but clert a God they's playin hurlin. Could that be right?

Suppose it could, Bart say, unable to hide his disappointment. An is this in the future?

Aye, an well intiv it, says she. About the same number a years as there's pounds in yer note. Now, I sees a fierce stylish-lookin fella, wuth the magic of a slide dancer. Jesus, he just after flickin the ball intiv the back of the Galway net.

This woman better not be bullin hus now, says Bart.

He's a lad wuth a Galway monicker too, but wearin a Offaly jersey. I can only barely make out the name. Fl … Fla … Flat. Someone wuth a name of Flaherty. I just after seein it in the crystal ball.

An what about the football? aks Bart.

Can't see any'hin on that at all, she sigh, but I sure that be some'hin solid there aan the hurlin. Can feel it in me bones.

This fairly well sober Bart in a hurry. He begin to huff an puff. It's the football I'm wantin to know about, he start to complain.

73

That's life, the Puckeen's missus remark wuth a sigh.

Like the darkie's left tit, me da adds.

Whadda ya mane?

It's neither right nor fair.

While this talk's goin on, I see the Puckeen givin his missus a nudge, unbeknownst to Bart, that seem to mean – Get back at it again ya witch. Give him any'hin – a good lie to get the gomey outa here, so we can all go an get a dacent night's sleep, an a aisy twenty pound note.

But she isn't normally on for rabusin the crystal ball. Accordin tiv her, it bring bad luck. Let me try agin, she says out a desperation when her husband give her another puck under the table wuth his knee.

Again everyone go quiet except for the dogs that begin bayin at the moon – a sure sign this time the magic isn't workin. The spirit or the force or whatever you call it just isn't there. The whole show turn intiv a sham, an everyone know it too bar Bart.

Still he start grumblin tiv himself. Shhhh she calls. Somethin appearin. Yis, but she's fierce misty. That's cause it's rainin cats an dogs. Croke Park, yis. There's the McNally Stand, an O'Hare's sayin Offaly's winnin by a pint, an Mick Casey's havin a stormer out in the middle of the field.

But Casey plays in the forwards, Bart's protestin.

O'Hare say they bring him out after halftime, she add, much to the relief of hus all. There's no flies on the Puckeen's missus.

Well maybe, says Bart, but he's lookin dodgy. What colour is the other team's jersies? he suddenly aks, tryin to catch her out.

She haven't a clue, but choose the furst colour that come intiv her head. Red is for danger, says she.

Jesus, that would be the Louth men all right.

There, she cry, the whistle's just after goin. Offaly's won be a pint. Isn't that mighty! Their furst ever Leinster! An there go the image – fadin – foggin over, an the rain teemin down.

I've a feelin yus is bullin me, says Bart, but fair dues to ye for givin me the opperunity for some late night entertainment. There's yer twenty pound.

Well, I'd put me money aan Offaly if I war you, say me da, who know only too well how tempermintal Bart can get. Like the wind he can blow hot an cold, or from any angle. That's why me auld man know he can never tell where he stand wuth Bartholomew Brock. All over you one day an rabusin you the next.

I can see the whole memory of that gatherin fade before me now in me own mind as I tell you this, Pecker, just like that pictur in her crystal ball.

# 10

In spite of the short night, me da have me up bright an early next mornin an out to Madden's we go for to do the few jobs. It don't take me too long after that to get below the Creeper's bottom board, not that I'm over excited to know it's jusht that we come upon things be chance which give hus a picture of the geezer's quare ways a carryin on.

Before father go workin for him, we already hear about his dog, Dingle, a Wickla collie wuth a hairy bum, his wool full a shitballs an a big slobbery tongue an clumsy paws full a play. He jump up on you an leave slurry marks all over yer clothes. Creeper love the fella. Dingle we is told he ushta kick the dure of his bedroom open wuth his front paws an lep up onto Madden's big double bed splashin shit all over the covers.

Bad dog, he cry out in helpless laughter, for Madden don't care a fierce lot about the mess til his sister start complainin. One day he come up with this great bright idea. To cure the leppin he get this extension from the lectric wire runnin in the field nearby brought in thro' the windie, an finces off the bed wuth it.

His sister's about ten year younger an live in the same cean as well, an look cruel like him wuth the same fat head. She love wearin them bum-huggers of skirts that war a mile too short for her, showin off her fat calves an thighs. She always wear white ankle socks – dirty ones I musht add – an she have a grin on her like a bag a chips.

Anaways this mornin an I strayin past this windie wuth the wire goin in, I hear this gruntin an gigglin, so I steal up close an take a peep. There in the bed is the two of them – brother an sister – wuth not a stitch on an they goin hard at it, like the hammers a hell, as if they be marrit. I can't believe me eyes it's so disgustin. I slip off about me business an never tell a word of it to father I is so ashamed, but I've no bother makin Goat wide to the quare tutter maloga goin on in Creeper's bed.

Later that day we is out among the turmic drills again – long rows a light green plants in high headland fornenst the blue smoky slopes of the Slieve Blooms, yer lower spine goin stiff an the backs of yer legs gone sore again from all the bendin – doin all the donkey work for the Creeper Madden who pay hus shag all. Pure slavery it is for the want a some'hin better in store for the moment, an me da swearin he won't be spendin the rest of his life doin this kinda work.

There musht be lots a betther ways a makin a crust, Whack. Here I'm labourin in this situation all cause of the feckin traipe. Let that be a lesson tiv ya now.

Durin the times he's managin to stay sober, things is a lot more robustical an he make plenty a garaid wuth the Puckeen Hussey in his day sellin waxie or tradin in horses, but the dreepers always do in his head.

There an then as I ruz to swipe away the sweat on me brow wuth a swish of me shirt sleeve, I make me own pledge that I'll never let the drink come between me an my own res'lution to make a good livin.

Another evenin Madden himself, his fat sister an the da an me is out viewin the corn in the field. Creeper's burshtin to relieve himself, so there an then he take out his pork soldier an start peein on his crop.

It's not as long in the shank as lasht year's, May, he say tiv his quare sister, but there's more in the head.

Definitely shorter in the shank, Matty, but thicker round the butt, would ya not say, says she, smirkin, an then winkin across at the two of hus. What you reckon, Joyce? she aks me da wuth a queer little sneer.

The heaviest ear's the one that lowest bends his head, ma'am, he say quick as a flash. This leave her puzzlin for a deeper meanin. Me da's sayins usually has.

Yer referrin to the corn now I suppose?

Of course. Still, there's many a thing with a high head today that'll be lyin low tomorrow.

Is you havin a slag at me, mister?

I'm only tellin ya the things I notice in life, ma'am.

Well you could say it in a different tone of voice then.

That one's even crazier an dirtier than her brother, Creeper, me da complain on the way home. He's in particular bad form this evenin. Some inner fight goin on within him over the drink, I feel.

Then this poor auld scarecrow of a fella come peddlin toward hus on a big black Humber bike, thin as the run thro' a gun, lookin like a corpse, an in spite of the close weather he's wrapped up in this heavy dark brown topcoat, the colour a clay.

Would any of youse happen to know the way to Ballynob cemetery? he aks hus.

An what's wrong wuth the one ya come out of? me da shoot back. That totally outa order now, his biggest weakness that ustha get him into trouble time an time again – he jusht couldn't keep a zip on his sharp tongue.

The awkward auld fella don't know what to say for himself after that tongue lash so he just get back up on the bike an as he's cyclin off I do me best to tell him the way.

When he's well gone up the tober, I lash intiv me auld man.

Don't know where ya get yer manners, but that not good form, misther. How in Jesus' name ya expect anyone to show respect for you carryin aan like that ta strangers?

Twas jusht one a them moods, he say starin me wuth his dead eye. Nothin else is said of it.

Another evenin I'm peggin turf intiv the big stone shed whin who come ramblin in thro' the open gate only Creeper's neighbour, Birdy O'Brien, his hair gone all thin an wispy, an a cute stubbly auld grin on him like Max Smiley for the Gillette razors. He have about as much hair on his chin as on his auld nopper.

By the cagey gimp, you know he not relaxed bout his intentions which make me prick up me ears all the more when I hear him chat wuth the boss next dure in the hayshed.

Them two auld sorrowful mysteries out the road I been tellin ya about before. Gilbert an Gertie – remember? – the ones wuth no runnin water nor lectric nor tilet, shittin in the fields jush like the knackers you has workin for ya for I've spotted their spraints in me ramblins, Creeper. Jesus, ya musht be mad ta have the likes a them tinkers hangin round your place. Sure wouldn't they rob the cross off an ass's back or the shite out from under ya even. Yis, you'd want to be screwin them right an proper fore they do it to you. An ya think they do the stealin themselfs? God no, Creeper! They tip their buddies off on the besht time ta make the strike. No, Matty, I wouldn't have them within ten mile of the goddamned place.

There's feck all of any use in this house they can shteal, Birdy.

No way would I let them in or near a farm, but that's up to you. Anaway back to our two buckos. He musht be the guts a seventy an have no pension book cause he no birth cert. Can't read nor write neither. Anaway, even if he could his eyes is cruel bad.

An outa the kindness of yer heart you've decided to give him a lend a yours?

Plus a bit a me grey matter intiv the bargain, Creeper.

I'm sure there's more than budgie seed in it for Birdy O'Brien?

Well, I is workin on his birth cert, an whin we get that end fixed up legitimate like, I'll pop it off tiv the social welfare, an be Jesus won't he be delighted!

How ya goin to get a legit cert when the auld boy's a bastard, Birdy?

Jesus, ya have me there. What I intend doin is work out his age from the auld baptism records in the chapel an hand that in.

An what's in it for you?

Plinty. Sure he's no kin, an there's his house, sheds, fine yard an twenty acres a rank virgin bog up the road, not countin the sixty acres he been squattin aan these lasht thirty year, yis? An he tell me he's no bank account. Still he been daylin in cattle these lasht fifty year, to say nothin about his mother an father before him whoever he was, yis, an they all too mane for ta spend a penny.

His mattress musht be stuffed wuth it, Birdy.

Well, I intend findin out.

Why ya tellin me all this?

Cause I can't do it all on me own, Creeper.

You lookin for someone crooked as yerself to seek advice an pay the bills?

I wouldn't put it that way.

What other way can you put it, ya snaky auld rat? It's you they should be callin Creeper an not me. An what's in it for Matty Madden I'd like to know.

Half of every'hin split down the middle.

Sure that work out at only a quarter!

No, I mane half the house, half the bog, half the land, half the savins? Yis, if you could pay the odd bill, then I'll do all the dirty work, an no one will ever know Matty Madden's involved at all at all.

A lot of mumblin an arguin go on between them after that. I can't catch it rightly. Still I feel I get the jist of almost every'hin, so I slink off for meself to tell the auld man.

He's mighty excited by me story. I know the cure for that pair, he say.

What's that?

Report the case to Father Mooney.

Sure he's worse. Don't he go be the nickname a Father Money?

But we'll knock mighty gallery outa followin the rabusin goin aan between them. Twould be a divil ta see who win, but any move we make toward that end get knocked outa course over our preparations for the big football match between Offaly an Louth in the Leinster Final.

# 11

Meetin this Louth team we keep bein told is goin to be no cakewalk. Sure didn't they win an All-Ireland in 1957, while after umpteen tries Offaly's yet to win a Leinster!

On the countdown to the big day neither the papers nor the radio gives hus a ghost of a chance. They won't have the bottle on the day, the reporters is all sayin. Outside the county everyone's backin Louth, an among our own folks Molly Hussey's forecast's beginnin to wear thin. All them boys who's inclined to see the bottle as half empty is claimin – If they didn't win one before now they'll never feckin win one.

Then I hear this talkin bout some curse or other that be put on the team ages ago by a thick cuinnic from the pulpit, an while that remain they'll never make a fist of it. Offaly's a team that's jinxed. Even Bart's thinkin long an hard about puttin money on them too, an he a diehard Faithful County supporter.

Makin hats an flags for the Louth boys is easy enough, but the green white an gold always take that bit longer. As for the crepe hats, me mammy, gran an Ribleen makes rakes an rakes.

Early on the big mornin, me da, meself an Ribleen heads off up tiv the Big Smoke. We gets up in plenty a time an park ourselfs round the Jones Road end of Croke Park, an when the crowds starts comin we get into sellin big time.

Just before the senior match begin we's totally sold out of every'hin. The crepe in them hats isn't much use in stoppin the grey rain fallin just before the ball's thrun in.

That wet'll favour the more dogged min, me da's grumblin. In no time I notice streaks a red green an gold runnin down the fans' faces.

Will the Puckeen's missus' forecast hold out, I'm wonderin, cause it's lookin fierce shaky at half-time, but just as Molly say, doesn't Mick Casey get moved out to midfield in the second half. Jesus, the signs is lookin good, an Christ why didn't I put money on it meself, I'm wailin now. Offaly puts in a fierce burst toward the end.

God bless you, Molly Hussey, Bart's shoutin at me da an they leavin the Cusack Stand, after Offaly's famous victory by a single point an their furst Leinster ever.

Oh you of little faith, Bartholomew Brock. Christ almighty I nearly renege on me own beloved county. Now I'm hundrets a pounds the wiser. The rain pissin down on his crew-cut head an he shoutin over at me da, Hey Block! How about the Offaly Inn later?

No better man, Barty!

Next he spots me. Whack, you're a chip off the best, he shout. Tell me son, is it really true? Or is it just a fairy tale? Come over here an pinch me, cause I can't fuckin believe it!

It's for real okay, Bart. No need to pinch you cause a that, I says nice an cool like.

Yahooooooo! come from the animal end in him.

There's a mighty stream of Offaly vehicles in a long line out the road from Dublin. Our van's right behind the Scutch Spollen's cattle wagon, painted green white an yella for the occasion, an packed wuth upward a twenty hardy bucks rangin from the teenage up tiv auld age behind the creels – jumpin wavin an roarin like balubas a whole load a them.

Passin thro Kildare there's plenty a begrudgin short grass boys wavin their lily white flags at hus for spite. Take care I don't go take a left turn an grab a few of yer woollybacks outa the Curragh, me da shout at them.

Once we pass outa Kildare an intiv Edenderry, the rain finally stop an a pale sun's filterin his way thro' thin cloud – the evenin light, the colour of champagne, a drink for champions. From Edenderry on there's bonfires leppin up everywhere. Even the rale sober element among hus is turnin intiv a gang a gomadoodles, me da say. Jesus, I nearly dropped when I seen Con Cuskelly, who's wore the pledge nigh on fifty year, pissed outa his head in Larkins.

Again we make for the Offaly Inn. Bart's loaded wuth deener cause of the huge great odds he get on our team. God bless ya, Molly Hussey, he keep cryin.

Who the feck's she? this auld nosy parker's aksin.

Tell me, mister, did you have money on Offaly?

Jesus, I seen them go down too many times before for that.

Oh you of little faith, an ya livin in the Faithful County? Is there no backbone in ya? What kind a fuckin fan are you anyway? Is you a man or a mouse? The crowd find this funny an from that day on he become known as the Mouse Brennan. Hey Block, over here! Bart shouts, nudgin Mouse outa the way.

We no sooner squeeze over when he wraps his arms round me da. Only for you, Block, I wouldn't a gone to that woman. God bless ya, Blocker Joyce. Not just for tonight, but come the morn an tomorrow night too! Multiplied by seven! Every day an night for the rest of the fuckin week – the beer's on me, Tinker man!

You want to see me da's eyes light up when he say that. Roll on the All-Ireland, boys! Bart's shoutin now an the rest of the crowd's cheerin, eggin him on.

Marge, the buxom beor, marrit but separated wuth three young childer, an a mighty country an western singer, come swaggerin in the dure wuth a fag in her red painted mouth, a bright green dress huggin her mighty arse an white cardigan squeezin in her fat tits, the yalla hair on her nopper makin up the third colour for the Faithful County.

Bet you'd rather be between her shafts than a bog barrow's, Block.

Sure, Barty.

Hey Goldylocks, Bart's callin. Sing us a good Faithful County song.

We don't have one, she say rale glum – not only cause of that for it's rumoured one of her kids is his.

After she have the babby, she go round complainin, Jesus I wouldn't mind but I'd them conterceptives took an all.

When Bart hear this he roar, Tis hard to keep a Brock down wuth a full bag, boys.

What we goin to do now that we don't have a good Offaly song? me da aks.

Be Jesus then we'll have to invent one, Block.

At that Bart put his arm round me da again an hug him hard. You know comrade, he says, his voice tremblin, this is the happiest day of me life, an the silly auld gomey start cryin again.

Next thing he jump up on a table, clears his throat to make a pernouncement. Hush folks, the Blocker's callin – Barty want to make a little speech tiv yis all. Quiet now, gentlemin!

What about me? Marge is shoutin.

An the lady as well.

She been rode too many times for that, some know-all shout from behind – a great big tall black-haired fella wuth elbows sharp as angle iron. That's as close as I get tiv seein him, Pecker, but I notice it bein well dwelled upon by herself an some thick butty fella later who I hear turn out to be her brother.

Fellow Gaels, says Bart. As you know I'm a man a few words. He coughs an hems then, clearin his throat. A true bogman in the dacent use of that particular monicker – in gimp and manner to the degree where you could safely say there's bog juice in me veins.

Jungle juice! Squinter Scully shout, gettin a loud laugh.

Thanks to me you makin a dacent livin. Saved ya goin to England, Squint, didn't I? Don't forget that next time ya want to top up yer dole!

That put Squint in his place.

Bart resume his spake. He get rale rosemantic like. Me breath smell of heather and bog myrtle, an deep below the bottom board in me, folks, is an Offaly man rare an true.

To all the Faithful County supporters – whether at home or in exile or abroad or in foreign lands or far from their native shore, or where else they might be – on the half of the true royal faithful contingent of the green white an yella in the Offaly Inn, I wish to suppose a toast for all our heroes on the field of play today. Now, folks, if I can get no seconder for this notion, then I'll second it meself.

I'll second that, shout me da.

Thro' the chair, Squinter shout. Put it thro' the floor. But no one pay any heed.

Lift yer glasses, mates! says Bart. Three cheers for our boys. Hip, hip!

And the crowd goes baluba. Hurray! they all roar.

Today our lads makes history. The pub's gone totally silent now for Bart as if the Monsignor himself in his black cassocks be deliverin a sermon. And me along with yis is the witnesses! Come on, ye Offaly boys! he cry out in a hoarse croak, an the crowd's roar nearly lift the roof off the premises. Roll on the All-Ireland, he shrieks, an we repeat it like parrots.

Anyone other than Bart in the whole county an he would have been laughed out of existence or told to shut up an cop himself on, but Brock have the stuff of the leader in him, or should that be a tyrant, Pecker?

Jesus, give hus a break, the Puckeen's complainin in our corner. Sure yis only after winnin an auld Leinster an if ye bate Down, sure Kerry will kick the livin shite outa yis.

That's the Kerry cuteness comin out now, me da's nudgin me. Just cause his own team's sick a winnin they could come a cropper.

Sing a good auld Offaly song there, Brock! Marge calls up at him.

Sure you's the one that tauld me we don't have one, Bart shout back.

Be Jesus I've one, say the Squinter Scully.

Get him up here then, Bart calls, jumpin down off the table, an the gang lift Scully up in his place. There's fierce calls for to keep the crowd quiet til Bart let out a bellow.

Finally, after a few coughs Squinter start his song:

*Come all ye faithful*
*Joyful an triumphant*
*Come all ye faithful to*
*The Off-aaly Inn*

Shut up ya gobshite! one fella call.

Blastfeemer! shouts another.

This is summer, ya bollix – not Christmas! Marge roars.

*

A good while after I meet up wuth Goat an we take a stroll down the main street. The people's out of themselves howlin, wavin the republican flag an singin, smoochin, drinkin an pissin wherever they feel like. God help hus if we's caught doin the like of this of a ordinary night, Pecker. There's a great big bonfire in the square an not a shadog in sight. Me an Goat gets plenty of ale intiv hus.

Early in the mornin we gets a lift home in the Puckeen's van smellin of shit from the dogs he carry cross the border up north. Goin in the back dure I look up at the sky. Cranin me head an twistin me lurogs, I'm makin out a gondola moon tossin in a sea a sparklin stars. A mighty day's had by all bar the men from Cooley.

That night there's no sign of me da returnin home nor is there any hint of him the followin mornin or evenin neither. In fact he go missin for the whole week. I hear a neighbour tell me ma he's keepin Bart company celebratin Offaly's glorious win.

That's rich of him, says me ma, an he a Tuam feen. Divil a good the Brock fella do for keepin him off the traipe.

The next Saturday night there's a fierce shamozzle wuth Bart in the Offaly Inn. By this stage he don't know what time of the day or night or week is in it.

Anyway in come Marge, an Brock try his luck in throwin the leg over her again, but of course she's havin none of it, cause there's no chemicals between them no more, Pecker.

Next up stroll her big butty brother. I'm warnin you, Brock!

Stay away from me sister if you want to know what's good for you. Ya poked there once too often. Buttsy put out his hand for to paw him away.

If you fell into a bunch of nettles, how you know which one stung ya? Bart say shovin him back.

Nettles? He's scratchin his head in a puzzle – not quite getting it. Pissed as his sister. The whole place in an uproar, laughin.

Yer man guesses right. This is a jibe intended at him an his sister. Jesus, but he draw back a fist at Bart's wide open jaw – remember Pecker, this whole job's bein done in slow motion – til me auld fella, playin good Samaritan again, steps between them just in time to receive the belt smack intiv his nose. That fairly sober him up in a hurry, I can tell ya.

Next day he come to in his nest, bruised, sore, not knowin how he get there in the first place, repentin for his sins til he get the hum a sizzlin rashers in the air.

Heard that one umpteen time before, says me long- sufferin ma, shoutin down at him in the bed fore turnin her back on him.

Let him suffer, she's shoutin intiv the pan in the kitchen. Ribleen, toss in them chopped onion too. That'll really drive him ruilla.

# 12

The followin mornin me an Goat rummage the dump beyant the helm an cart home rags, glass jars, porter dreepers, duck down outa an auld pilla, horsehair pult outa a scrapped harness, an an auld mattress wuth a rat's nest in it.

Before settin out to fish, I pick maggots outa a rottin hen that I find in a drain. These I puts in one a the jam jars. Me an Goat, well us entertain ourselfs mighty all durin that summer. A sally rod or hazel, a bit a thread an a pin hook tied on. No fancy rods for hus cause we don't have the price a them.

So up on the piebald pony we get, me wuth a tight grip on bit an reins, an have her goin at a steady trot, wuth Goat hangin on behint. Down the path we go leadin tiv the woods happy as Larry an free as the wind, clouds a fluffy cotton driftin cross a sky of forget-me-not blue, sweat drippin heat an a fair chance a thunder. A mighty condition for the fishin.

Tome for a trout, I says tiv Goat.

That river too shalla for maggots or worms, Jack. Mevvy we do a fit of the hand fishin inshtead? I show ya.

So we tie up our horse an crawl down on the bank of the fast-flowin stream.

Put yer hand down like this.

Goat show me.

Feel aitch side of the rock. Rale aisy do it. A bit like feelin

90

yerself in the dark. Aisy now, Whack, an ya touch him shiverin there. Tickle him nice an gentle til yer other hand come for ta make the grab, like this, an fore I know it he's one lifted wrigglin in his hands an land him on the bank like a miracle. Mighty peck for a pavee, Whack?

I'm too stuck for words to say any'hin. When it come to tryin it meself, me fingers isn't fasht enough. Goat get an odd number a three outa bout ten feels. I musht a touch round ten, but get nothin for me trouble.

An Jesus, of a Sunday too twould be mighty chasin hares or ferretin rabbits. The like of a half three-quarters hound or any'hin near the like, an you can make a go at the hare. Failin that the ferret's worth his weight in cartridges.

Other times we goes snarin. Makes the snares ourselfs. Check the rabbit's runs in the hedges. Set your snare an tie on tiv yer peg hammered well intiv the ground an cover it wuth grass.

Safer than narkin chickens, Jack?

Arra forget them snares an lamp them be night wuth yer car battery in a bag wired tiv a headlamp, an a good gun dog well-trained who know whin to hauld back. Of a dark an windy night me father often kill forty or fifty conies an sell them in the shops.

No point in all that now, Whack, wuth d'auld myxie.

It's while we's hand fishin Goat aks me if Birdy makes any more visits tiv the Creeper Madden.

Mevvy, but none that I sees or hear. Jesus, there's some rotten scene goin on there, I says, referrin to Gilbert an Gertie. Is there any'hin we can do for them poor auld buffers, Goat?

I be on for ya to go tiv your auld friend Joe Joe furst, he say.

I reckon that be a tome idea. Next day we meets wuth him.

91

There's some'hin funny wuth the wirin in that Birdy man's attic, he say. Could never warm to that fella. He about as sliddery as a eel an never have a good word for anybody. Bent me ear onetime about all the bollixes he have for neighbours, an go on an on complainin about every one of them.

Jesus, they can't all be bad as you're paintin them, I says. God, he's mighty put out, Whack. Don't like it one little bit – me cuttin into him like that.

Then Joey tell me how Birdy burrit his wife, an she still a young woman. There's lots a rumours goin round he gave her cruel beatings, Joe say then, an it wouldn't surprise me if it didn't have a mighty deal to do wuth her goin to a early grave. He's a rat, an I bet he's up to no good wuth Gilbert an Gertie. They is aisy bait for the likes a that rogue.

Is there any'hin we can do to help them? I aks Joe Joe.

Well yer father's suggestion isn't a bad one. Father Mooney's a better man by far than the Birdy O'Brien.

You reckon I should go see the cuinnic?

It mightn't be a bad way a cuttin that bollix outa the action fore he get too big a foothold.

Tell me, Joe Joe, how come he by the name a Birdy?

He was baptised Bill. Growin up he used to be a hoor for Bird's jelly deluxe, specially the strawberry flavour. Goin out he bring a box an ate it concentrated in the picturs. Meetin him outside after you swear he war wearin lipstick. Some sight, Whack.

Mevvy he look more like one a them vampires that be just after suckin the blood out of the neck a some poor innocent girdle out in Hollywood?

That would be more like his form.

Me an Goat gets tiv discussin these matters between

ourselfs. Goat's a great one for draggin out things. I is more for divin intiv the thick of it.

I tell you, says he, let's mooch round the two ceans an we'll come back an report on what we see. There may be more tiv all this than meet the eye.

So we agree that I keep an eye on Gilbert's cean any time, mornin or evenin when I'm free, while he do the same round Birdy's.

*

Gilbert an Gertie live on their own a short ways outa town in this rale backward spot on the edge of a great big hill. All I have to do is climb up on one side an then steal down a short way tiv the great thick hedge wuth a big gap in it. An believe it or not if I war to crawl thro' that gap I'd end up on the roof of their turf shed for she's built right intiv the side of the hill – in an auld sandpit that get dug out over the years.

They's the greatest way a bringin in turf ever. The driver he bring the tractor an trailer intiv the high field, an all they have to do is take the galvanized an makeshift rafters off the roof an then yer man back the trailer up tiv the edge an tip her in. No handlin at all. A mighty manner a drawin, Pecker.

Right below me now is Gertie herself, an Jesus, you want to see the get-up of her in an auld ragged dress an a dirty grey cardigan fallin off her, loadin mangolds into a rusty pulper, an she up tiv her ankles in mud in her wellinhans. The smell comin up to greet me – off auld rotten turmics an pig shit out of the other shed – fit to lift the peck outa yer belly. There she is turnin the handle, an singin away tiv herself – the slices fallin in a heap on the ground. Fornenst her is the back of their wreck of a cottage wuth this huge bunch a nettles growin well up over the sill of one of their bedroom windies, as good as any blind. How a buffer could put up wuth such shite an dirt's beyant me.

I is no sooner settled intiv the ditch when I hears this tractor pull up at the front of their house. Of course I can't see who it is, but I don't have to wait too long, for who come waddlin inta the yard only the Birdy himself, carryin in one hand the full of a yalla bag of – as it turns out – clothes. Bein nothin better than a pot a slop himself, I know he have no trouble comin to grips wuth the horrid pong.

I see ya brought me laundry, says she out thick like.

It's nearly time we moved them cows, Gertie, says he, down to them back fields. They's fairly well shaved the grass where they at this minute.

You know what's right sure enough, says she. Did ya get me pinsin fixed up yit, Birdy? she shout out rale sharp at him.

I keep gettin on to them, but they're fierce slow in these government departments.

Curse a friggin hell on them goberment crowd – keepin a feckin auld cross-patch like me waitin. What do they expect me to live aan – fresh air?

That not even to be had in Gertie's yard. She lead the way toward her back door wuth Birdy followin. An ya tell me a bank account would make me money? I could just about hear her aks the cute auld hoor, fore they is outa earshot.

No point in me stayin round ana longer, I says, fore crawlin outa me hide an goin back home, figurin Birdy have the two of them for whatever little fortune they might own. Pretty well sewn up, I reckon, an there isn't much that I, nor anyone else, can do short a robbin the geezer.

When I gets home, Goat's waitin, burstin to tell me his end

of the story. Jesus, there be no way you get in there, he say. He have two great big alsatian dogs tied onta huge long leads – one guardin the front of the house an the other at the back – an a rake a signs warnin ya again trespassin. Ya wouldn't dare go near them for they'd chaw a leg or a arm off. She remind ya of that place in the cowboy pictur we see one time in the Savoy where they keep all them gold bars. Fort Nox or some'hin like that? They's the two most vicious-lookin beasts I ever come across. Now if ya believe it's important enough for hus to take a look in there, I knows a great way of puttin them to sleep. What ya reckon, Whack?

Wouldn't mind havin a gloak, Goat.

Then go fetch me a few yokes.

Knowin Goat, I've a fair idea what he want, an sure enough I see both of them things in one a Creeper's sheds, so I goes an gets them for him that evenin.

Fierce early next mornin Goat take out two full pound a doctored sausages split even into two brown paper bags. Next we set out on our little walk to Birdy's farm, hidin ourselfs in a ditch near the avenue that's bare but for the tree stumps. The minute Birdy get the farm intiv his name, don't he go an mow them all down. It mean he not have to cut turf for near aan seven year, tho' they say it take from the look of the house, to say nothin bout all them pisherogs agin knockin down such lovely fine trees.

As we crawl farther down long the hedge, gettin closer to the cean, that savage of a dog mindin the front get the whiff of our scent, an come growlin in our direction. Hearin how mane this Birdy fella is, we know he's already likely to be vera hungry, so when he get as close as the rope allow, all I has to do is toss him a bag of the raw sausage, injected wuth weedkiller, while Goat race down along the ditch to feed the cur guardin the back of the cean the same dose.

Goodbye dogs, Goat say, racin back, an we disappear across the fields, without as much as a growl from either, they's so eager to gulp down the raw poison.

We keep a close ear to the ground all day long for word about his alsations. Next mornin I hear in Flynn's shop they take sick an the vet's sent for, an he have to put them down.

Later that day all hell break loose, wuth Birdy accusin the well-known jogger, Peter Jones, for this mane cruel act. A month earlier Jones is runnin past yer man's farm when one of his dogs break loose an near rip a ligament outa his leg. Jones go tiv the guards but the sarge don't want to know any'hin about it. That's a civil matter, he say. You may go to yer own solicitor about that. Next thing he threaten to report him to the *The Offaly Independent* when Birdy refuse to pay him compo.

# 13

Next evenin I see Birdy goin intiv the barracks in a fierce state. I goes lookin for Goat, but he nowhere to be found, so I takes the chance a moochin out round Birdy's on me own, knowin he won't be back for a while yet. I hasn't a clue what to expect when I goes knockin on his front dure. I'm not sure if he have a family or any'hin. When I get no answer I goes round tiv the back one, but get no reply there neither. I'm just about to walk away when I think I hears a faint cry comin from somewhere inside the cean. Me ears prick up like a collie's. Yis, it sound like a girdle's voice callin out, Help me, please!

Hauld aan, I says, comin in the back way. I tear thro' the kitchen intiv the hall. Where is ya? I cry.

Behind this door here.

I turn the knob but the door's locked. He keeps the key in the jug on the dresser in the kitchen, she cries. Hurry on an get it. Please!

No bother. Hauld yer hault, now, I tell her.

Openin the door's no problem, but what I see behint it frighten the livin daylights outa me. Sittin there on a bed in the middle of the room should be the grandest-lookin beor you ever clamp eyes aan if she not a been bet black an blue round her oglers, cheek bones an mouth, an down long her legs as well.

Jesus, who do this tiv ya? I aks.

That mad auld lad a mine, she whisper thro' a pair of very bruised lips.

Jesus, he ought to get the jail for this.

There'll be little fear of that, she say.

All the time I'm keepin a close ear out for the sound of his tractor. Why he bate ya like that for? I can't help but aks.

He done a deal wuth this rotten auld cur down the road whose land's mearnin ours. Two hundred acres or other, an he promising me auld man a brand new car and over two thousand pound if I marry him. But I'm only sixteen, an he's sixty-six! That's fifty years older than me. I don't know how often I try runnin away, and the auld lad haul me back each time. You'd want to see the beatings he give me.

I can see wuth me own two eyes.

He's hopin the auld fella will shortly kick the bucket, leavin us with all that land. I'm in fierce trouble. I must get outa here – away from all these greedy crazy people. The problem is there's no one close by I can trust.

Did ya go tell the guards?

Of course, but the auld sarge tell me he can't interfere in family matters. Me father knows what's right for me, an if I get a beatin, sure I must a deserved it!

An did you go to the priest wuth yer problems?

Sure, and he tell me how this old lad's very highly regarded in the parish, an he'll treat me with the height of respect, not like those other young randy cowboys gallivantin round these days. An me father's very shrewd and highly regarded as well, an can only have my welfare in mind. Go home and think about it, lass, is his partin words to me. I'm telling you all this cause I'm desperate, tho' I've no idea who you are, or what made you call by.

I give her me monicker an say, Oh, I just come by beggin, that's all, pointin to me basket a goodies.

This may be me only hope, she says tiv me then. But I've no money and no way of getting out of here. Would you ever be able to help me?

Be Jesus I will, I says, makin her a promise. Leave it with me, I add, hearin the din of a tractor in the distance. I'll work on it straight away, an have no fear. Sometime tomorrow I'll be back wuth news, so hold on tight til then.

At that I dash out, lockin the dure, an run down the hall intiv the kitchen, plonkin the key in the jug an out the back porch in a flash an clearin the ditch just ahead of the tractor pullin intiv the yard.

Then I goes an tell me da every'hin, includin the bit bout the shadogs an the cuinnic. Jesus, that's a fierce state of affairs, says he, for that poor girdle to be trapped in her own cean, an then to be spancelled to an auld goat like him for the rest of her born days. The things them buffers gets up ta, Whack.

That's fine, I says, but what we goin to do to help her?

Twould be too dangerous for hus, me dad say then. If we's seen to be helpin her, then her auld fella an the shadogs they be all down aan hus like a ton a bricks. Blocker here would get all the blame. Jesus, how the auld sargint would love that!

Sure all ya need do is give her a lind of a few deener after openin the dure whin the auld fecker isn't there. Give her an address she can go to for to get her bearings, an who be any the wiser?

Me dad stand considerin this for some time. An would you mind crawlin back in there an doin them things?

No problem.

Yer not afeared a gettin caught?

Nee'r a fear in the wide earthly world, I say, tellin a lie.

We have to keep it dead secret.

Sure.

What is you so sure about?

Bout keepin it secret.

From who?

Just bout everybody.

Bar who?

You an me.

Who else?

Don't know.

Well I do.

Who then?

Everywan else. Yer mother, Ribleen, yer Pavee Club pals – blood bonds or no. Everywan – for all time.

I think about this. It mean I can't tell no one ever? A dark secret like the king wuth the horse's ears in that auld yarn me granny tell me?

Yis, I says. I understand.

Then we'll try for this evenin.

Me da go off an gets some money. Then he go intiv Tellamore an call Uncle Eaney, his brother, in Ballyfermot up in Dublin. That show you how much he trust auld Stacie, the postmistress!

That evenin I goes back moochin wuth me basket. I see what look like Birdy out in the fields toppin thistles wuth his tractor, yet I is not a hundred per cent sure, cause I has eyes like a hawk. The hump on the back thro' the jacket look familiar but the hook nose – that ain't right – so I'm sniffin up near to the windie of her bedroom furst, when I starts hearin this shoutin an roarin an bawlin. I duck down an keeps me ears peeled.

You're nothin but a brazen little hussy, just like yer auld one. Look what happen to her for her trouble – pushin up daisies in yon graveyard! Birdy's goin baluba wuth Cora.

Which show how much respect you've for her memory, cause it's the only grave not minded. That's why there's daisies!

Keep this up an you'll be joinin her!

I'm not puttin up with this any more.

Where you be goin this time? Now for me next trick I'm about to disappear! But where – in a small parish? Up someone's chimney? Maybe in another haystack like the last time me an Sarghint Gillick root you out. Go ahead, girl. Who'll take ya this time? An ya just gone sixteen. By law it's me that's in charge. I'm yer legal guardian. Go aks the guards. See what they've to say! Look, I'm tryin to be reasonable wuth ya. Two hundred Irish acres of the finest upland in the whole of the County Offaly mearning me own! Sure yer man be wearin the wooden overcoat in a few short year. Then look at ya. One of the best-heeled lassies in the whole Midlands. Just think a that.

I want no part in yer scheming. The whole thing's wrong from the word go. It's not right. I'm not going through with it.

Well I'm tellin ya you is.

I'll go through no ceremony with that dirty auld—

Be Jesus you will! Even if I have to handcuff you an put ya in a straightjacket an keep ya locked in here an drug ya to the gills. This is the chance of a lifetime. I've raised sucklers with milk bottles, plucked dead calves out of cow's wombs wuth these bare hands here – hands that could strangle ya this minute without as much as thinkin twice about it, you brazen little hussy! I've broke in wilder fillies in me time! There's one thing you've got to learn bout this world. In this neck of the woods it's the man that makes the decisions. In your peculiar case, it's your own lovin father.

A silence linger long enough for me to notice me heart beatin like mad.

Where I is hidin I see nothin, but I've no bother hearin what happen next. There's ferocious ructions. The sound of the thumps would sicken ya, an the wails outa her is some'hin fierce. I'm about to jump up an make a beeline for the door an have it out wuth that dirty bollix. Still if I do that he'll be aan tiv me an she might never escape. Next I hears slaps that sound like he's usin a leather belt on her.

Jesus, this is deadly serious business, I says tiv meself. Some'hin's goin to have to be done. I crawl out an dash over the ditch like a buckin hare an down longside it tiv the tober, too excited to notice the fragrant whiff off the honeysuckle in the hedges. Me da's waitin rale cool in his yalla van pullin in a deep draw a Ruthland's plug tobaccy in one of me granny's dudgeens. I hop in the passenger side an tell him to drive outa here like the hammers a hell.

I've no intention, he say. That only draw attention tiv ourselfs.

When I calm down I tell him what happen.

Be Jesus, that's totally beyant the beyant. We must try it again tomorrow evenin, he say. Will you be willin to crawl in again?

Definitely beyant a doubt.

Next evenin fore we drive out, we make sure Birdy come intiv the helm first on his tractor for his usual nightcaps. When we gets to the fields me da say, You better act quick.

I creep in long the same way as the evenin before til I is facin the yard. I crawl up tiv the windie again, an give her a wave. By her face I can tell she's delighted to see me. Get me out please! I hear her call out.

In double quick time I'm in the door. I grab the key out of the jug an let her out of the room. Jesus, Pecker, I nearly drop dead when I see her. How the bastard can get away wuth this bates me. One eye on her is gone all bulgy an ruby, like on a dead hare hangin up be the legs. Will she ever be able to see outa that again? I wonder, thinkin of the story me da tell me on the way down to Killorglin.

What done that? I aks.

The brass buckle on his belt.

Imagine that hittin ya in the eye, Pecker! Only she's lucky there isn't that little squirt a fluid like in me da's case.

She scrape up a few of her belongings. I lock the door an put the key back in its place just like nothin happen. We leave by the way I come in. Down along the ditch we creep, crossin the fields to where the van lays waitin in a misty twilight. I slip Cora into the back an hops intiv the front, me heart thumpin, an off we head toward Dublin at a nice steady speed.

What Cora tells hus on the way up is some tale of woe I can assure ya, Pecker. The cruelty she go through be some'hin else. Any court of law in any dacent God-fearin land would throw that connivin bully in jail for life. May he burn in hell til kingdom come an let that only be the start, I says tiv meself in the van.

Suppose you hear of the fairies takin young childer? me da say to lighten up the conversation after hearin a near repeat of his own horror. Only this time, Cora, it's the Travellers that's doin the robbin.

As usual there's shag all traffic on the tober this time of evenin, an we make it into Ballyfermot no bother. We leave her in the hands of me Uncle Eaney. We'll find a job for her, he promise me da.

There's enough in that good deed to lasht me many's the year, me da say after leavin a very grateful girdle wavin hus goodbye from me uncle's doorstep.

Remember, he say, not a word about this tiv anyone, cause if you do we's frigged. If the shadogs comes near hus we know nothin, you hear? An he tell me what to say if they do come. It's important we both have the same yarn, son, an just in case, we better go get ourselfs a good alibi.

What's that when he's at home?

Yer Uncle Seamus out in the molly do hus fine.

Next mornin there isn't a word about her breakin out, but me da's sure it's only a matter of time fore the shit hit the fan, an he's dead right too. That afternoon the squad car pull up outside our cean an out hops Pork Chops.

The sarghint want a word wuth you, Mister Joyce, he say tiv me dad.

Suppose he's too lazy to come spake tiv me himself?

That's why he's provided the Paddy's taxi here. Sure what more do you need?

I take a lift wuth you, an people be makin out I'm guilty of some'hin. If yer sarghint want to see me he better come here hisself. Now good day to you.

He shut the dure on his face. Ten minutes later Gillick come knockin. Where were you yesterday evenin between the hours of six and midnight? he aks me da on the doorstep.

Well if ya want ta know, me an Whack here goes pickin mushrooms out in the fields.

Where?

Out near Birdy O'Brien's.

An did ye pick many?

Divil a one.

Did you spot anything suspicious near the house?

We don't go near his house, Mister Sarghint. One thing I be worried about tho'. I see a fox in one of his fields. If I war Birdy I be keepin a close watch on me chickens.

That's nothin for you to be concerned about. Where did ya go after that?

We go tiv me brother's camp for an auld chat.

Well, Mister Joyce, I'll need to bring ye to the garda station for some further questions.

Can't you do it here just as handy?

We're better set up for it in the barracks, an I'll need to ask your son a few as well. I'm sure you're aware that a girl went missin yesterday evenin?

Sure isn't it the talk of the place?

In the end we's no choice but to go down tiv the barracks wuth the auld bollix. Next thing, he's separatin hus. I'm kept sittin in a room at a table all on me own, wonderin what's goin on til I hear great commotion thro' the partition. Grunter's shoutin at father. Next I hear a mighty lock a thumpin an jostlin goin on an the partition gettin the odd rattle amid a load a wailin. Jesus, it sound like me da's gettin another fierce corripin. I sit there cringin in fear while all that's goin on.

Next the sarge come in huffin an puffin, his forehead gone all sweaty. He come over an bend his wet ugly auld puss near me ear. Well I'm just after hearin ye were involved with that girl yesterday evenin. Isn't that true, young Joyce?

Be gob it's not, I answer. We never seen the poor girdle. In fact I never clamped eyes on her in me whole life.

Your father says ye took her away with ye in his van yesterday evenin. Tell the truth now an shame the divil.

Isn't I already tellin ya the truth. What more ya want?

Well that's interestin now cause yer father's only after admittin to it out next door. I'll grant ya it wasn't easy got out of him, son, until he got a good few belts of this lad here. At that he pull out a black rubber truncheon that look like one a them dildos you see in those dirty magazines nowadays, an says, A few sharp thumps of this fella on the back of the neck an shaulders works wonders, lad. He admits to it long before I get down near the backs of his legs. Jesus the calves is a mighty place for getting a confession. It's amazin how a little pain can get to the root of the truth, tinker boy.

Knowin me auld man, I reckon the sarge have to be coddin me cause he's too stubborn to give in that quick, an I'm not on for lettin him pull the wool over me own eyes that aisy.

Now, boy, since you're not willin to co-operate, I want you to stretch your arms out on the table an lean forward.

I don't want to, but see no other choice. Then rale loud into me ear, he hollers, How come yer father admits to givin her a lift an you deny it?

Cause me father's a liar, that's why! I shout back at the fat bollix.

At that he lash the truncheon into the back of me neck. A smart of pain an I'm seein stars. I leps up at the Grunter an shout out, Kick a dog on the ground an he'll bite. Do that again an you be sorry.

You're callin yerself a dog now, Joyce? What breed a cur are you anyway? Hardly be any of the thoroughbred in you?

I stare into the big bully's eyes. Jesus, but they have a dangerous look in them.

Sit down here again before I whip you across the floor and out the door there an down the street in front of all the townsfolk. Sure you're nothin but vermin. No different from them foxes only ye think you're more clever. Wouldn't life be very borin in this auld kip if ye weren't around? The farmer shoots foxes for kicks, while tinkers are my bloodsport.

He ruz his truncheon again to give me another welt when Pork Chops bustles in. The super's on the phone to you, sarge, says he, so off he waddle leavin me an the shadog together. There's a awkward silence. Pork Chops shuffle over. Did ya spill the beans yet? he aks me.

I've no beans to spill.

Your father admits he give the girl a lift in his van an you were right there along with them. Now unless you own up as well, we'll have no choice but to keep you locked up in our cell til the judge passes sentence on you.

What can he sentence me wuth?

With not tellin the truth about bein present when yer father give that poor girl a lift.

Be Jaysus, I'll admit to no such thing cause that's not true.

At least I see a bit a give in Pork Chops. His pale cheeks goes limper an his eyes look downcast. Where did ye go after the mushroom pickin? The way he aks that I knows he's runnin outa fight.

We go tiv me Uncle Seamus for an auld chat.

What time was that?

How would I know? I've no watch.

Don't get shirty with me, fella. Was it still bright or getting dark or what?

The more he keep goin on about this, the better I feel, cause he's weakenin on the matter of the lift an that give me hope that they's bluffin me about what they claim me father say.

It be getting dark, I tell him.

And what were ye talkin about in the camp?

What's this got to do wuth the poor girdle that go missin?

Never mind that – just answer me question.

I hasn't a clue. I fall asleep, I says.

Pork Chops' white cheeks gives a little wobble an he let out a sigh, a tell-tale sign he's gettin nowhere wuth me neither.

Next thing the big auld pork belly himself come burstin thro' the dure followed by me father, lookin the worse for wear. Huffin an puffin as usual, the Grunter squeals, The two of ye get out of me sight an if I ever catch either of ye in trouble again I'll bate the livin shite out of ye.

What we do wrong? me daddy aks.

Come on, out! He rushes forward, wavin a threatenin hand.

That's a fair question, Sarghint, I says. What exactly we do wrong that gets hus inta trouble?

A case of givin a dog a bad name, lad. Then it stick with ye. You'll always be the first to get the blame for everythin that happen in this area.

Leavin the barracks, Gillick say tiv me da, Think yer smart now, don't ya, Blocker Joyce, but I've me strong suspicions yer up to the thick of devilment in this caper, an I'll get to the bottom of it yet. If I find you've any hand or part in this, I'll skin you alive. As things stand, I has ya for litterin an bein found on after hours. I'll keep houndin you, Joyce, as long as there's breath in me body. To an early grave if need be. See you in court next month if I don't see ya before that.

Now you see how treacherous that sly auld sarghint is? me da say on the way home. He'll use any way, fair or foul, to screw a fella. If you'd caved in an spilt the beans, he'd a gave me another fierce corripin. So fair plays tiv ya, lad. You show great courage, specially for a boy your age an considerin the pressure you be under.

By the sounds in your room, you be under savage pressure yourself.

Oh he skelp me plenty on the back of me neck an shaulders an then the backs of me legs. Jesus, tomorrow I'll be black and blue.

Try as hard as they could, Gillick can't come up wuth any'hin linkin me or me da. She just vanish inta thin air, an nothin more's heard of it, apart from what I hear about the beor's fiancé. I come to realise how we take a savage chance. Milly is suppose to be very thick an upset over it.

# 14

A few days later Noddy come tiv me wuth a excitin bit a news. Guess who the Grunter have for dinner in the hotel last night? he aks.

How's I suppose to know?

Him an Birdy O'Brien sit down to two big fat juicy steaks an ya know why?

I hasn't a clue, Nod.

Seein what you's been tellin me bout Birdy, I makes sure to keep close tiv them durin the dinner. I'd brush past an bend down pretendin tiv be pickin up a piece a dirt off the carpet or drop by to collect a dirty plate or set a table nearby. All the time I lookin the other way an hummin a tune tiv meself, but me ears is pricked. Words like bog, turf, grass an cattle gets lots a mentions, Whack.

Up at the bar later on I get me pal Bugsy to keep an ear open for what they's sayin at the counter. When I sees them gettin ready to leave, I goes out ahead of the pair intiv the tilet an locks meself in one of the horse boxes in the hope they might come in for a pee, an be Jesus they do. Gillick's sayin how they'll have to get Gilbert to claim for squatter's rights – then he'll make him get a will wrote out an have every'hin signed over in both their names.

Noddy's pal Bugsy tell him they spend their time talkin about Gilbert. Some'hin to do with his land.

So Birdy's gone an got the law on his side?

They's plannin on sharin it between theirselfs after the auld pair dies.

What can we do?

This is one for the Pavee Club. How bout tomorrow night? I'll tell Goat.

We meet the followin evenin. Noddy for a change have nothin new on offer. Of course me an Goat already knows what me da suggest, with Joe Joe thinkin it a vera good idea, so I mentions Father Mooney to Nod. Jesus, but he go ruilla.

After what the Reverend Rigney do tiv me in the sacristy, five year ago, after servin mass? An now ye want to help them to that auld buffer's money?

Who else ya suggest?

Noddy's stuck for a answer. The gomey won't leave it to any friends we know, he growl.

In the end we agree it might be better to get Father Money interested, an let them battle it out. Whichever way it work, twill be at Gilbert an Gertie's cost, but then you can't bring it wuth ya, or as me granny say, the property of the miser often end up in the hands of the spender.

In this case they is more like chancers.

No way they'll ever leave it tiv a shower of minceirs, Goat complain an we leavin, echoin what Noddy say earlier. In any case we agree that I go straigh away in the mornin to see the cuinnic an try bate the other two tiv the game.

When I gets home I tell me da the whole story. He's ragin when he hear bout Grunter. Be Jesus, I'll go see the Monsignor meself, he says.

You cut no ice wuth them sky pilots. Let me go to Father Money. What better way for a man that's mad to be made a P.P.

than by offerin him a way a raisin plenty a garaid for the new chapel?

Suppose, you have a more innocent look tiv ya, tho' you's been losin a fair lock a that since comin intiv this feckin helm.

Together we goes over the way to break the story tiv the cuinnic.

When I go to see him, I'm told he's gone to another parish for a funeral mass an won't be home til evenin. Walkin past the barracks I notice the sarge pullin away in the squad car an headin up the town. Bet he's goin out Gilbert's way, I say. So I make a dash, takin a short cut across the fields, til I arrive at the gap overlookin the backyard. Sure enough the Grunter's car's parked out front. I hear voices right below me in the turf shed where himself an Gilbert's dodgin the shower that's lashin down on top of me.

That summons over the lights, that'll be thrun out too, Gilbert.

I take it you an Birdy will put in yer own cattle.

All your worries about rearin cows will be over. You can sit back wuth neer a worry in the world. Sure the rent we give ye along with yer pension, twill leave you right as rain.

All I hear outa Gilbert is, Yis, yis, followed by – Suppose it's as well to have the law on your side, but he's not comin down firm one way or the other. Gillick won't be slow in firmin him up, I'm reckonin.

I need to see this cuinnic, I say, leavin the field. When I knock that evenin, Father Mooney answer the door. A beefy-cheeked man, his neck's so fat you swear the dog collar's about to choke him. Mevvy that's why his face is so red. This time he wear a snarl on his face. Suppose the hoor's wonderin what this useless pavee want wuth his time.

Hear you lookin for a lock a money to build yer new chapel, I says, gettin tiv the root of the fruit.

And you're coming with a big lump for the fund? he say kinda saucy like.

We just win the sweep, Father, an we's wonderin back home how much we should give for the chapel. Have you any idea?

You're pulling my leg?

I'm afraid so.

How dare you waste my time then?

Fore you tell me to get stuffed, I has some'hin worth considerin, Father.

What's that?

I'd rather be tellin you inside where it's nice an private, if you don't mind.

What's this all about?

Money, Father.

Jesus, you'd want to see his eyes widen. They didn't call him Father Money for nothin, Pecker.

Wavin me into a quiet room just off the hall, he sit me down at this fine table wuth a white lace spread cloth. He begin to soften me up nice an smooth like for openers, aksin me bout me family, how they's settlin in an things. I tell him everythin's grand an rosy in the garden.

Then the chat come to a full stop.

You say you've a suggestion about money? he aks.

Two people I knows, Father, I tears intiv it mad eager, that's up in years an if all the gossip's true they's no livin relations. An two well-known min in the parish is tryin to do them outa their little lock a land an house.

How you happen to know all this?

113

Be a pure accident. I come across the two rascals chattin one day in me moochin.

Moochin?

I mane beggin, Father.

The cuinnic don't look too convinced. Who are these two?

Gilbert an Gertie Sweeney out the road.

Up on the hill?

Spot on. His lurogs brighten an his nostrils flare like a stallion's. You swear he's gettin the sniff of the deener already, Pecker.

And who are the two rogues?

Oh they's vera well got in the parish you be surprised to hear.

If you'd to put up with what I hear in the confessional, Jack Joyce, nothin would ever surprise you. Two upright gentlemen you say?

That's if you care to call Birdy O'Brien or Sarghint Gillick gentlemin, Father. There's people I knows that wouldn't.

No rushing to rash judgements now, lad. What makes you think these two are up to no good?

Cause I hear them talkin, I says, tellin him a little white lie.

And where was that?

Behind the ditch fornenst O'Brien's house.

What was it you hear, son?

Birdy have Gilbert's money locked away in his own bank an they's agreed to split it between them if the sarge come in with him on the racket. The house, land, bog, every'hin they'll divide in half. Birdy have his own cattle on it already an Gillick's bringin in his own next week. They's settin about gettin squatter's rights for Gilbert. They already payin him rent, an when he die twill be left tiv them in Gilbert's will.

114

Not a bad arrangement, Jack. No mention at all of Gertie?

She don't get no mention, Father.

Still there's nothin illegal about helpin somebody even if it's aimed at helpin themselves later. No court can find fault with that. You hear all this behind a hedge?

On me word of honour that I may drop dead, I says, hopin it won't happen.

Why are you telling me all this?

Couldn't Gilbert just as aisy leave it all tiv the church an be sold in God's good time to help pay off the loan on yer new buildin? Wouldn't that fine high field mearnin the town make a grand site for yer new chapel, Father?

By God, Jack, you'd make a mighty accountant, solicitor and auctioneer all rolled into one. What size fee will you be charging me for all this?

Not a penny. It's just that down the years we always have it in for the auld sarge. He never do hus ere a good turn. Indeed every chance he get he try to do hus a bad one.

So there's an element of revenge in your intentions, Jack, he say now – the rale cuinnic comin out in him.

I suppose, Father, I have to admit, sorry I ever open me mouth about Grunter.

Tut tut, son. A sinful thought you're harbouring there, and it's my moral duty to point this out. Next thing he aks, Does anybody else know about these people's plans?

Not another sinner apart from meself, I says, tellin another little white lie.

Jack, leave this with me. I'm most grateful for your help, and you mightn't believe this but I did have Gilbert on my list. Your information will make my visit all the more urgent. Perhaps I'll see them this evening. With luck, we'll come to a little arrangement. Sixty acres, a cosy cottage and a prime site for our chapel – how many plenary indulgences could you buy with all that? A huge remission of time spent in purgatory! Now remember, son, what I say about harbouring thoughts of revenge in your heart.

At that he show me tiv the door. You'll let me know how you get on, I aks, not too hopeful he will ever.

Thumbs up in the street if I'm successful, thumbs down if I'm not. How about that? he say, nearly knockin the teeth out of me head with him slammin the dure in me face. That's cuinnics for ya, Pecker. Heads stuck in the clouds when they's talkin to minceirs.

# 15

Good times I suppose can't lasht forever an the first sign they's about to end come one day wuth a knock tiv our door. The sargint send up a shadog to tell father that his lad Whack have to attend school come September. He also make a visit to Goat's da as well wuth the same news for his son.

The followin day the principal of the vocational school in the town come to the dure wuth a form, this big tall boney lookin geezer wuth a nickname of Boner. This I guess is cause his surname's Bonner.

The sight of him make me da fierce thick. What makes ya think me son want ta go tiv yer auld kip, he aks. Jesus, ye musht be fierce short of pupils to be comin beggin ta Travellers?

Father don't realise it then but he hit the nail on the head. Boner's in a desperate way to get his numbers up.

He'll go tiv the Brothers instead, me da say.

That's rich comin from a man who doesn't even go to Mass, auld Boner sneers fore goin next dure ta get Goat to sign on. Suppose he know more about what goin to happen than father, cause when he go down to see the Brother he tauld they's full up. Anaway your son would be better off in the vocational school. Don't they do metalwork in there? But he not sure if it's tin or steel they use, which me da take for an insult, an he's dead right.

The followin day I meet Joe Joe in the street an tell him me tale a woe. He find it all fierce amusin. You see the sargint's sons is attendin the Brothers. That's why he get on to Boner. He don't want the sons of Travellers mixin wuth his own. Also he know he must enforce the law, an every dog in the street know that the occasional school need numbers. Ya see, Whack, I know how their little minds work, an that auld Brother up there's a snob. He won't rock the boat. If I were you I'd play it nice an easy. Sure you're free as a bird to do an go where you like.

There's a crow perched on an ESB wire above hus an Joe Joe chattin. Jesus, Joey, wouldn't it be grand ta be a crow. Fly over every'hin. Look down aan everyone?

But that's the beauty of it, lad. You can be like that bird. If the whole set up in this town gets too much, you can always get up an fly away. Now don't get me wrong. I'm not recommendin that til you come of age, but that's the one big advantage ye Travellers has over us. Now, son, let's play a little game with these auld guards.

She's a tight squeeze, but me an Joey get inta the nearest telephone box.

He slip the few pennies into the slot and ring this number he know by heart.

He get me to listen rale close tiv his ear.

There come this loud boomin voice.

Can I be of assistance?

It's Guard Fitz at the other end.

Yes, Guard, Joey say, givin me a little nudge in the ribs, I'm in fierce need of a screwdriver. Would ya know where I might get one quick like?

Hauld on til I see if we've one here. Have we a screwdriver handy, Sarghint? I can hear the auld gomey callin.

118

Find out what he want with it first, we hear Gillick shoutin back.

What you want it for anaway? Pork Chops aks.

I need it for to break the box here to get out the coins.

Who are you anaway? he aks, when Joe Joe slam down the phone.

There, he say, just a bit of entertainment from the most serious pair a men God ever put on this earth, after the Monsignor that is. Next time we meet we'll give it another gander. I've plenty a tricks up me sleeve for them boys, son.

*

This threat of school have me sorely frettin, Pecker. Of course I go tiv the national school the odd time but at the age of fourteen I believe I be done wuth educatin.

Look, son, me da say this day, spottin me worry, yer brain's a bit like a fusebox. Get it too fretted up an you overload some of them fuses, an pop one a them little wires goes, an you end up wuth a stroke or a heart attack or some'hin. At yer age the only strain you should be feelin is just below the belt of yer trousers. Look, lad, don't take this schoolin ta heart. It part of the price we must pay for bein settled. Make the odd appearance. An occasional school, isn't that what Joe Joe Meagher call it?

He then go on to give some advice. One thing be sure an do in that place, lad, is learn yer sums. There's Travellers knockin about who think they know it all, but they's not half as clever as they think. They gets swingled in dales cause they can't add proper. Remember auld Missus Ward in the molly beside hus last spring? Well she go inta Flynn's Hardware to buy some waxy. Why she don't go an buy it off one of her own's beyant me. Anaways this cute hoor behind the counter say, Sorra ma'am, I make a hawful mistake there. Eight yards at nine shillin a yard, that's eighty-nine shillin an not seventy-nine as I say previous.

You'll give it ta me for seventy-nine? the auld gomey aks.

I'll tell ya what. We'll split the difference. How about eighty-four shilling? an she leave thinkin she get a bargain, all cause she haven't a clue how ta do her sums. Get me message, son? Be sure an learn yer tables.

For the length a time I spend in school up til then, it's a miracle I is able to read an write an do the few sums. When I put me mind tiv it I can pick things up rale fasht.

Definitely I coulda make a doctor or a professor or some'hin. As for the readin, I pick up a good lot a words in the bubbles outa the picturs in the comics. The Bash Street Kids, Lord Snooty, Roger the Dodger. Only for them I be pig ignorant when it come tiv the readin.

*

The day we's dreadin finally come, when me an Goat gets sent up tiv the tech. Any'hin like the gawks they give hus an we goin in thro' the front door is some'hin only a Traveller would understand, Pecker. You'd swear we's savages an I'm sure they honestly believe it.

Welcome to civilisation, boys, Mister Boney Arse say tiv hus in his class. You know, when I can't take the bog out of these dopes what hope have I takin the tinker out of ye pair a dudes? which ruz me hackles I can tell ya, but then what hope's a young lad wuth a big baldy buffer of a bogman like this gent?

Tell me Joyce, he say tiv me this day, where were you educated?

I get plenty a headucation in a good few places up an down the country in me own good time, mister.

Headucation? You mean in a hedge school? he aks rale smart.

No boss, I get it belted intiv me nopper wuth a book d'auld teacher pretend to be readin.

Well me an Goat we doesn't get on too well wuth the young scuts in this school at furst. There's a fair plenty bit a sortin out to be done at the breaks. Goat's a mighty help in this department. It's not be accident the Puckeen Hussey's king of his tribe an Goat have the forkin to be blessed wuth a set a fists like his auld man's, which the little shower a buffer an townie scuts knows nothin about til some a them gets foolish enough to start gangin up again the likes a hus out in the yard, Pecker.

It begin innocent enough. You might get a jostle passin a lad or one of the wise hoors try trippin you up from behind. Then there be name-callin an slaggin. The biggest bully go by the name of Teevan – a little prick in me an Goat's class – remindin me of Dennis the Menace, wuth broad shoulders to match his big wide mouth. Full a guff too wuth a big rough head an black wiry hair bristlin like a jack's brush – the whites of his fists knucklin for battle.

I isn't inclined to creel the ignorant little stoomer. No way is I goin to turn him intiv a martyr at me own expense.

How can you tell when a tinker woman's havin her period? Teevan aks me an Goat one day – the crowd gawkin at hus waitin an answer.

When she's found to be wearing only one sock, Teevan say wuth a smirk.

You mean when she turn her toerag into a jamrag, another smart arse aks an they all burst out laughin.

What goes in an out, in an out, in an out, an smells? he aks then.

Me an Goat shrugs our shaulders.

Six knackers doin The Siege of Ennis, Teevan says. Again there's a rake a laughs.

What happen when you put a tinker on horseback? Teevan aks hus next.

Again we've no answer.

He'll ride him to hell, says Teevan.

This time there's no sneerin. Suppose it's cause the others don't quite get it.

Another day, in front of his own crowd, Teevan aks me an Goat, Have ye many dogs at home, lads?

Goat, takin this as a innocent enough question, say his family's rakes of them.

And you, Joyce?

We's a fair few. Ya bollix – I'm sayin under me breath.

Then that explains it.

Explains what? Goat aks.

If you sleep with dogs you'll rise with fleas.

So?

Isn't that why the two of ye is forever scratchin yerselves?

As usual this get a flutter a giggles.

You'll want to watch what you's sayin! Goat say back at him rale thick like.

Put a zipper on it, I whisper in his ear. We'll get this bollix good an proper in our own time an place.

How often does yer auld lad beat yer auld one? Teevan aks me next day on the corridor. This time he's on his own, an I answer him wuth a right smart puck in the gob that fairly well quietens his tongue, but it don't go anywhere near curin the little prick.

Instead, he choose his own time, makin sure there's plenty of his pals round so he'll be safe, when he start slaggin.

Teevan's slaggin come in for a lot of discussion at our next meetin of the Pavee Club. Isn't it funny but I gets on great with him, says Noddy. But I know a way that'll put manners on that townie. She's a mighty long shot, but maybe tis worth a chance.

What's that? aks Goat's Tail.

How about a little bit a rat baitin long by the stream here next to Fennessy's where there's rakes a nests. Teevan's been bendin me ear about goin to hunt for them. He looks up to me. Thinks I'm a great fella, Whack.

How's that goin to put manners on Teevan?

Bring a terrier, Saturday afternoon, an we'll learn this guy a thing or two about rattin, Noddy say, leavin hus none the wiser.

Well me, Goat an the Puckeen's best little ratter's waitin for them to arrive that lovely warm sunny Saturday. Next we see them crossin the field. Nod's carryin a spade, Teevan's empty-handed.

He introduces hus to Teevan like we don't know each other. This time tho' he's fierce friendly. Didn't know ye was Noddy's pals, he say. Then he pause for a gulp of air fore resumin, I'm willin if ye's willin.

Willin for what? I aks.

Let bygones be bygones.

You mane all that slaggin in school?

Sure.

All right by me. How bout you, Goat?

Jesus, that no problem at all.

But I'm Goat's friend long enough to know better, an he's well able to read me thoughts as well.

Now lads, Noddy give the orders. Goat and Whack – ye

scour the grass bank for escape holes an any ones ye find be sure an mark them. Me an T – we'll check out this side of the stream here. Any hole we'll block with stones an mud so they'll not be able to escape into the water. That okay, T?

Can't wait, Nod.

That's what I love about you, T. You're full a beans. We'll take off our shoes an socks an roll our trousers up now, cause we need to wade in the water here a bit.

I notice a look of alarm on Teevan's gob.

We really have to get into the stream?

Look I'm doin this since I be a lad a seven. This is the only dacent way of managin, isn't it lads?

The only way, we says in a chorus.

Teevan's reluctant at furst but when he see Noddy take his brogues off an then roll up his trouser legs he follow suit. Next thing they is in the stream blockin up the rat holes, while Goat give me a little nudge an say, Noddy come down here yesterday evenin an he know exactly what he's doin.

It's still a mystery to me, I complain. Nobody ever tell me any'hin.

Be patient, pal.

Next thing they is back on the bank. Noddy's all business. Got to work quick now fore they – pardon the expression – smell a rat. Stand over here out of the way, T.

Noddy direct him to stay at a spot next a mossy rock juttin out of the ground. He get me to back away too in a different direction. Goat have a hault of the terrier by the lead now an they follow Noddy over to the river edge just above one of the blocked rat holes an he start to dig down. When he reach the underground tunnel, he continue to follow it away from the stream. Not a stir out of ye now, he say, an the terrier lettin out little yelps.

There's rats here all right. That's what Browser be sayin.

As the farmer said when he cut the dog's tail, It won't be long now, says Goat. Stand still everyone. We're nearly there.

Noddy says, Keep the dog's nose outa that tunnel, Goat.

In a flash this big fat ugly brown lad creep out of the hole in the grass beside the mossy rock an right behind where Teevan's standin. Wuth nowhere else to hide an smellin the dog, he see no other way but to make a dash up our lad's leg. Next thing lookin down in alarm Teevan spy this big lump of a yoke streakin up the inside of his trousers, his scaly claws pinchin intiv his skin.

Oh Jesus! cries Teevan. Next thing he's screamin an shakin his leg like crazy, hopin he'll fall off. By this stage the bugger's head's probin his y-front so he can crawl in an take a nip out of his mickey. God be good to them townies that could afford to wear drawers, not like in me an Goat's day, Pecker.

Lucky for Teevan he's wearin a tight pair. Findin his way blocked, the rat make a u-turn and dash down the way he run up. Teevan's face go deadly white.

Meself an Goat's enjoyin this huge, though I'd hate to have it happen to me, I can tell you, Pecker. After landin back in the grass, the rat make a beeline for the water. A spectacular lep off the bank. In a flash the terrier's on tiv him. His jump's even more amazin, snappin him outa mid-air wuth his jaws.

Teevan he get the fright of his life, an they tell me he still have nightmares over it to this day.

# 16

In the few months we's in the cean I begin to wonder if it's worth it all, an it's gettin me hot an bothered. This thing about settlin, Goat, we argue on the way home from school, what will the likes of hus get out of this in the end? Draw the dole. Live in the wrong end of town, get treated like shit. Jesus, Goat, me lingo's changin even.

Yer beginnin ta suffer from settlement pains, Whack, but you'll get over that.

Settlin into what? That's what I'm aksin ya.

That's up to you.

What you mane?

Two choices. Turn intiv a cakesham or stay a cream cracker. If you don't like it, you can travel the road, biy.

Jesus, but you's getting fierce stuck up, Goat.

Course I know why as well. Goat's the Puckeen's son, king of the bare-knuckle boxers of all Ireland – bruised nose, battered lurogs, gums for teeth. He look the part an all. Goat, in the Puckeen's coat tails, is randy for a big jump-up in life, an the helm's the place for that. Try an be like a townie. He knows the girdle's eyes is lit on him too all over the terrace. A firm arse, back like a plank, muzzly arms, head curdly an handsome. A fine broth of a boy.

Still Whacker Joyce isn't too far behind. Just cause his da

have only one lurog, Whack's a tome moocher. He'll carve a name for himself too. Sure all he have to do is copy Goat. Tag in along wuth him an see how he be courtin his tome beor from the terrace – Annie Murphy.

Chestnut hair, black cherry eyes, brown skin in summer. I know how twill turn salla in winter just like me sister Ribleen's. Still there's some'hin about her I don't like. She's far too stuck up in herself, actin just like the Red Sea ought to part for her every time she walk down tiv the shore, just like it do for Moses in that picture of the Ten Commandments we see in the Savoy. What she have to be stuck up about's beyant me.

She never say much. She don't know any'hin about a sense a humour. When others is laughin, she stands there sulkin cause she didn't cause the laugh. A stuck up bitch an a right pain in the arse, Pecker.

An Goat's braggin to me about her. Jesus, Whack, she take all her clothes off for me the other evenin in Feery's shed. Oh Christ she's gorgeous. Ya know what, Whack?

No. What?

She have enough hair on her fanny to stuff a horse's halter.

What colour is it?

Well, this is the God's truth. Different to the chestnut shade on her head. I not tellin ya a word of a lie. It's as red as a fox's hole.

I'm at a loss, cause I never see a girdle naked in me whole life, but I is cute enough to know this much. That mean the hair on her nopper's dyed, Goat.

Ya reckon?

I'm sure so.

Goat don't look too happy. You notice the pair a hips on her, he say back. Fit to breed like a haggard a sparrows. I'll be the biggest babby-maker in the whole county yet.

Goat, you's a good bit wiser than me in the ways of the world, I says, cause you in here a good year longer than hus an yer father's the king. You don't mind tellin me like how ya make out wuth them girdles in the helm?

Just watch my moves, Whack, an you'll learn a fierce lot.

My little question make Goat's day.

\*

Another way I put manners on Teevan come be a pure accident. Not only that, it change me life as well in a big other way. One day I bring me pet ferret inta the class for a few laughs. I has him in a box in me school bag. When yer lad Teevan's sittin readin a book, I slips the ferret inta his jacket pocket. In no time he snake out on tiv his lap an nips him in the bollix.

Lookin down he leps up howlin. Another rat! he's screamin.

The ferret run across the flure an then the girdles starts shriekin an jumpin up on the desks an chairs. There's fierce ruilla in the room. Lucky we is havin a free class, an be the Lord Jesus we have plinty of them in that auld kip. No wonder no one want to send their kids there.

Then Sally Kelly, a lass me eye's beginnin ta widen on, start slaggin Teevan, an they all end up havin goes at him, which he don't like one little bit, while I slips over an lift up the ferret in me hand, an this cause another round a ferocious screamin.

This little ferret give me fierce power over them townies. So long as I don't rabuse it, an there's no doubt they see me in a different light after that. Indeed, Sally call me a notorious knat, which bring a smile on me lips she like enough for to give me a hug.

She have lovely thick long yalla hair like a tinker's an grand peanut-coloured skin. Every'hin pretty on her come in pairs.

Two cute dimples when she smile, an a lovely pair a big round green eyes, an a fine pair a buddin breasts inside her cardigan. Then that pair a long shapely legs that seem to go on forever, stickin out of a rale short skirt their skin the colour an nap of a brown eggshell.

A lot a fellows is lustin after her, like Luke Luby, the gomey wuth the crooked head. His mother have a hard time wuth him at childbirth – gets starved of oxygen or some'hin. The wirin in the attic isn't up to standard, or as me da say, he have space to rent upstairs. Sally would only be prick teasin him, puttin her hand on his thigh close to his mickey, or blowin him a kiss an then winkin at me behind his back.

The ferret do the trick. He put manners on Teevan. Sally take a shine to me. Isn't it lucky we both happen to be in the same day? She tell me afterwards she like me rugged looks – that babby face, pug nose, fair curdly hair an big eyes like two plump sloes in a ditch. Says I'm easy goin but hard as nails an fears no one. Says she feel safe wuth me. If she only knew the truth, Pecker – this townie's world have the livin shite scared out of me.

From that day on I get the measure a Teevan, an the others see me as a bit of a character.

In the afternoons I walk Sally back home tiv the terraces. The stares you get off some a them women in the helm. Take a look a that pair, the Widow Mooney seems to be hintin. Just like water, doesn't tinkers always find their own level?

Cream always rise to the top, ya ruilla auld witch, I growl under me breath.

What brought that on? Sally aks.

Readin the mind behind that sour auld puss'd bitch over there. Don't like the way she's lookin at hus, that's all.

Jesus, Whack, you'll want to control yourself. Maybe you can read her mind, but say that to her face, you won't have a leg to stand on. She'll win hands down if that ever go to court.

I take yer point, Sally. I be a bit of a gomey there all right. Anyway there's some'hin personal nigglin between hus. Me da says, Anatime you catch that look, son, keep sayin tiv yerself, We is the true raw Irish, an we's too close tiv their own sad past for their comfort. Always keep that in yer brain, lad, an the pain will fade. Like the donkey that bore the Saviour inta Jerusalem, we has a heavy cross to bear, Sally. Would ya agree?

I get the gist of what yer sayin an that look you're talkin about. Like we's pure shite or somethin? Sure I get that all the time. I don't give a feck what they think, I keeps sayin, but if you want to know the truth, I do care, Whack. Looks can cut right thro' to your heart, an hurt an make ya feel little.

24 Ashfield Park, where she live, is no oil paintin. The red dale windies rottin, paint peelin off the walls, green scum on the gable end, fascia crumblin, the front lawn like a meadow.

Jesus, I could mow that for ya wuth me pony, I says for a laugh.

She don't find that very funny. Only things is in a bit of a mess inside, I'd invite you in, she says.

I reckon it can't be half as bad as our kip at home, but I'd a loved to look inside her cean an see what it's really like. Still I is half a kind afraid of her auld one in case she'd run me altogether.

All day now I'm drummin up the courage to aks her out, but I never seem to be in the right place or, failin that, the time's wrong. A bag of excuses, walkin in fear of me own shadow. That's how snug I feel in this big townie's paradise. I'm down tiv me last chance for this day at least, anyhow. Some night you wouldn't mind comin to the picturs wuth me? I manage to aks her in a rush, tho' a lot of that get stuck in me throat.

At the weekend. No bother.

Where will I see ya?

Outside the chippers, Friday night at eight.

It's like a lectric shock's goin thro' me, an me hair feel like it's standin on its ends. I get butterflies in me stomach, an goes off me food when I gets home. That night she's constantly on me mind.

I'm skinnin this big silver eel in the kitchen sink of a evenin when there come this awful bangin on our front dure knocker. Me ma open it.

Hello, Missus Kelly, I can hear her say tiv the woman. Do come in. We's about to have a sup a tae, only we don't have mugs – just jam jars. Would ya like a sup outa one yerself?

But this lady have her airs. No thank you, she decline. I'm here about a most serious matter, Missus Joyce, an it concern your son. He been pesterin me daughter, Sally, during an after school hours an I want it to stop immediately, you hear? It's hard enough tryin to rear me own without havin the likes of your lad interferin in the upbringing of me girl. Sure there's no manners or rearin in him at all. Walkin round the town all times of the day and night. I want this interferin to stop, Missus Joyce, you hear?

I hear right enough, Missus Kelly.

Look, we all know he can't help bein the way he is, God love him, an he didn't pick it up off the ground either, Missus Joyce, I can tell you that. More to do with the way ye go round rearin your young ones, but I'm sure you'll appreciate, I don't want any of it rubbin off on me own girl. Is that okay with you, Missus Joyce?

I'll be sure an pass on the message, Missus Kelly.

I'm burstin to make a dash to the dure an face down the auld cow, but me feet feel like lead. I can't get them to move, an there I is strugglin to lift them. Then I see Mrs Kelly peerin in at me, but she have the Widda Mooney's head on her, when I wake up in a sweat. What kind of a stupid auld dream is that? I aks meself. I'm in a awful state, til I try to talk meself out of it. Look fella, I say, sure you haven't even seen this Missus Kelly yet. So what ya goin aan about? Jesus, how I ushta hate them kinda nightmares, Pecker.

# 17

Another thing Sally do for me. I begins to enjoy goin to school, but it's only on account of her. It ushta kill me when she wouldn't be in. Still I notice she come more often too.

On account a you, she whisper in me ear one day.

Still I know these feelins can be very tricky. I'm nothin but a notion in this poor girdle's nopper, an that could turn in a jiffy, an I'd be some flash pavee then, eh? I have a lot more to lose outa this arrangement than her. Clert to Jesus, she's me Marilyn Monroe – me Hollywood queen? Even tho' I know the mushes in the nicer parts of the helm sees her as a piece of trash like meself.

The pictur for that Friday's a John Wayne western. Goat's girdle hate them kinda films, but he's burstin to go see it himself, besides he's curious about me girdle. I know damn well he fancy her himself, so he come along wuth hus. I spot the grand smile on his lips. Like a dog wuth two mickies. The nerve of him.

Travellers loves picturs havin to do wuth horses an cowboys, Goat explain tiv Sally, swishin his red quiff back, an we goin in the dure of the cinema. I say we kinda turn her off with him doin so much bullin bout cowpolks durin the filum.

We goes an sits up in the back of the balcony. There's courtin couples all round hus, an they don't give a shite what the pictur's about, they's so stuck into suckin on each other's gobs.

I wouldn't mind tryin it wuth Sally, only Goat have to go an ruin it. When the filum goes a bit dead, he start complainin, Cowboys they's supposed to know all bout horses, but the crowd that make that filum knows nothin. I mane to have them racin like that in hot weather without fumin or steamin – who is they tryin to cod? Then goin on for miles without end like that without restin – Jesus, that's goin beyant the beyant. Ya know what, Sally? he say then, to get her attention off a me an on tiv him. Sure me an Whack we'd make our home on the range no bother.

An what would you know about cows? she aks.

Spot aan, I laugh.

Sure we'd learn about them in no time. Isn't they a lot dumber than horses?

So? Sally aks. And what makes ya think *you'd* be able to manage on the range?

Take one good look at them. Hasn't they got wagons like ourselfs so they can travel light? An we all look like them cowpolks too, wearin the same class a clothes an all. They goes huntin for their peck just like hus, an they entertain theirselfs wuth yarns an songs, an drinkin whiskey, an they's mighty at the bare knuckle boxin.

Will ya shut yer gob over there, ya scut? this big thick buffer call over at hus, or I'll close it wuth a belt!

It keep Goat quiet for a while at least. He lean over at me again, when I is cuddlin closer to Sally – Them mustangs I be astin ya about, Whack? Do yer father know any'hin about them?

Shut up auta that. I'll tell ya later, when the pictur's over.

Later over our plates of banners an sausages in the chippers, Goat gets back tiv the filum. The Duke Wayne, isn't that some rompin man? he aks hus. Sally don't look too impressed.

A rale travellin cowboy pavee, swaggerin along there in his high leather boots wuth spurs stickin out, an a cowboy hat, an the leather waistcoat wuth the sheriff's badge, handkerchief round the neck, an big thick leather gun belt with holsters, an two knobs of revolver handles stickin out. He's my kind a pavee, Whack.

An Maureen O'Hara – ain't she a tome beor for me cowboy man? Them huge eyes an gleamin teeth. Jesus, I love the way he give her arse a smack. What's yer name, gal? Goat try to imitate the Duke.

Virginia, Sally says. Virgin for short but not for long, givin me a sweet-toothed smile. You and your cowboys, she say then. If you want my opinion, I think ye Travellers is more like the Injuns.

What you mane by that? Goat aks.

Sure the buffers an townies see ye as balubas. Isn't they always putting ye down? Isn't your camps and haltin sites kind a like Indian reservations? And then ye go haywire when ye drink firewater, and yourself – Goat's Tail – sure that name's pure Indian, to say nothin about Whack, which I'm sure could pass for one too.

Get outa that, Sally Kelly, Goat says, sorely hurted.

What's the difference between Goat's Tail or Dove's Wing or Wolf's Claw? Isn't they all grand Indian names?

There's no flies on Sally Kelly. She fairly put hus to thinkin about ourselfs that Friday night in the chippers. So you don't see hus bein close tiv the cowboys, then? Goat's sulkin.

Well, I'll put it to you this way. If that's how ye see

yourselves, what would either of ye have to offer this squaw here?

Dunno, bring ya down a step or two, mevvy. Depend on how you see hus, an what bein wuth one of hus would do for you, Goat's still frettin.

The light from the globe above, for all its harsh glare, is a cruel test on her phizog. High jaw bones – lovely goldy hair, a cute nose, lips made to kiss. Jesus, me Sally's some stunner.

We bid goodbye to Goat at the turn on the tober tiv her house. On the doorstep I give her a soft pog. God she's so grand.

Mother's gone out. Come in for a minute, she coos in me ear.

Inside tis lovely an clane wuth a sweet fresh smell. No flies buzzin, no rabbit skins hangin, an they both sleep upstairs. A pictur of her mother on the mantelpiece when she seen better days. Still she look tense an on edge in it. Where did I see that face before I is wonderin, an dreadin to think what she must look like now after hundrets a bottles a vodka clocked up on her meter.

She make me an herself a cup a tea, an we sit there in the quiet of the kitchen. Then out of the blue, she say, Whack, I'm goin to let you in on a little secret, and maybe you already know. My late grandfather Jim Kelly an his wife Noneen was Travellers.

Jesus, if I hadn't a been sittin I surely have fallen outa me standin.

An what name do she have fore she get marrit?

A Stokes outa Roscommon.

I'm relieved to hear that cause for a split second there I'm in terror we might be in some way related, but I know there's no Stokes in our family tree.

So we's kinda connected? I says, tryin me best to keep cool.

We'd the same customs, Whack.

Jesus, I shoulda known by that fine yalla head a hair yer wearin there.

Whack, before I bid you goodnight, I'm goin to invite you upstairs. You can watch me getting ready for bed if you want. Afterward I want ya to go home. You're clear bout that?

Yes, I whisper, me one-eyed ferret beginnin to stir at the prospect. This is goin to be some'hin totally unusual. The sight of this lovely girdle strippin? Jesus, me heart's poundin.

She don't care a damn. I might as well be invisible an she standin there before me in front of a full-length mirror while she slip out of her skirt. Jesus, her legs have an end after all windin up in the curves of her lovely arse, an her skin's so brown an smooth like. Christ, I'm pantin, her knickers white, huggin her butt cheeks an she say, gawkin at me in the mirror, while she's groomin her long flowin hair, That's what I like about you, Whack. You's not one bit like the other fellas. Even Goat's too much of a wise arse. You know what I love about you?

Jesus, I hasn't a clue. I'm too charmed to answer.

You're sweet an innocent still. I feel safe with you. You're a sort a wild child. One of Nature's own. Tis a way I'd love to be myself. Before I ask you to leave, could I ask how you feel seeing me like this?

You is the first girdle I ever see naked in me whole life.

And ye all livin on top of one another in the mollys?

The Travellers is very strict bout that kinda lark, Sally.

Whack, kiss me goodnight. She bend down to take me peck on her cheek. Jesus, her smell tis some'hin lovely an delicate like apple blossom.

I go out on the landin, look up, an there I is starin intiv the piercin eyes of Jesus with the bleedin heart an the little red lamp glowin beneath it – his sharp oglers followin me everywhere keepin a close watch – better nor any house dog, specially if you's religious.

I fly down the stairs an out the dure wuth me in a flash in case I comes across her auld one. On me way home I tries to map out the road ahead wuth Sally as me mot. What would I have to offer her like? This child a nature as she like to call me.

Would you fancy this idea enough to run away wuth the Whacker Joyce?

But to where?

Whatever tickle yer fancy. Sure that's the beauty of it, Sally. An auld van wuth a caravan in tow an the world's yer oyster!

What about a toilet? I hear her furst complaint.

In behint the ditch. A minor detail, Sally.

For you but not for me. An there's no shower nor bath?

Can't have it every way, Sal. These is sacrifices you has to make for yer freedom. You's lookin for jam on both sides of the bread. Look on the beauty of the countryside.

Me mind flash back tiv that magic summer's evenin as a child lyin on me belly on the floor of me da's cart, its spoke wheels churnin up a cloud a dust on the dirt track behind hus, blood tinted from a red blazin sun settin below the horizon, leavin a trail like one of them comets you see blazin in the sky.

Not me cup of tea, Whack, I can hear her say. Never mind the summers. It's the winters I'm worried about with the cruel cold, to say nothing about all the rain an muck, an damp. Ugh!

I can see her turnin up her pretty little nose all right at this way of life. There isn't really very much I can offer the girdle, an this makin me sad on me way home.

# 18

As well as bein principal, Master Bonner's also our metalwork teacher. This big wiry Buffalo come from down Rosenallis way. A pity he so thick, cause metalwork's one a me favourite subjects.

The slaggin he give the class is some'hin awful. Me an Goat we's put in wuth all the gomeys in the 2A6 class an tho' I'm clever, I miss a savage lot a time an I'm usin that as me excuse for bein put in wuth the gomeys.

Aha, says Boner tiv me one day. We've one clever fella here – the young Traveller chap. Here today gone tomorrow, eh? Isn't that right, Master Joyce?

Yis, Mister Bone. No, I says instead, Yis, Master Bonner. I don't like the smirk he throw me then at all at all. Guess you need to be a woeful thick cunt to run a school the way you's runnin this one, Mister Bone, I mumble under me breath.

What's that you're saying, Joyce?

Nothin, sir.

Bone have his droll ways there's no doubt. When he get cross wuth hus in class he shout out some'hin like, If there ever was a itchin epidemic in the parish, you crowd be the furst to die cause yis is too feckin lazy to scratch yerselves. Teevan, have an essay for me tomorrow mornin – three pages a foolscap on what my world would be like without metal, and you, Joyce, on account a being a peculiar case, I'll allow you a little liberty. Three pages on what my world would be like without tin.

You say sin, sir? An the class start gigglin.

Don't start acting the tinker with me, Mister Jumped-Up Johnny Come Lately Joyce, he bark at me rale thick like, an the class go deadly silent.

How you expect me to write three long pages aan some'hin I not sure on?

Cause of your poor attendance record, Joyce, and seeing the tin trade isn't what it used to be – sure what else could have brought ye into the town – I'll make a further allowance with you. When you run out of ideas on tin, write a bit on plastic instead.

Can I write on plastic too, Mister Bonner? Teevan aks.

Strictly metal, boy, or I'll be doublin it.

Can I use drawings, mister? I aks.

Providin they're no bigger than a penny postage stamp.

How many a them can I use aan one page, mister? Either that or the way I'm callin him, mister, prove to be the last straw.

In writing, Joyce. For nine in the mornin, and no pictures.

No way Whack Joyce is goin to waste his time doin that class a exercise, an I tell me da this too that evenin.

Couldn't agree more wuth ya, says he. Yer in there, lad, to learn the few sums an a bit a readin an writin. That's it. Come wuth me tomorrow ta Creeper's. I could do wuth a extra pair a hands for the next couple a days, an whin ya go back, sure it'll have all blew over.

Jesus, I is delighted to be outa that kip, even tho' Madden's farm wouldn't be in me top ten a favourite places to be in either, but as it turn out it give me the chance to ketch a bit a conversation between Creeper an Birdy about their friends

Gilbert an Gertie. I have to climb like a cat up onto the hay loft to hear what they's sayin below.

Well, I finally got to the root of the fruit, Matty.

Where is it?

You're right. He have it stuffed inta his auld mattress, but there's one major snag.

He won't hand it over?

Not at all, an there's stacks of it.

Ya never bring it down here so we can divide it fair an square? Remember our dayle the last time?

Well it's not as clear-cut as all that, Creeper.

Then spit it out, an ya better have a good reason.

The fuckin auld mice have a huge pile of it ate.

Yer not serious.

Once they nibble off a serial number, the note's not worth a shite, Matty. It's as pure as that.

Hundrets a serial numbers ruined. Lovely pound notes, fivers, tenners, twenties – all gonners. Only good for wipin yer arse, Matty, an isn't that a God hawful waste a readies? Clert a Jesus I didn't know at the time they was useless, tho' I had me suspicions. I run like a maniac wuth me bag a nibbled notes inta the bank. Not worth a damn, the auld manager says to me, once the serial number's disappeared – just one digit – an they's dead ducks. Ya know that, Creeper?

Of course! What ya take me for? An eejit like yerself? An ya know what you wint an done? You has just advertised the whole show. Every Harry, Dick an Tom in the parish will know what yer up to, ya eejety auld bollix. Ya know what yer sufferin from, Birdy?

Yer man stand there like a dummy.

It called foot in the mouth.

Look here, Mister Madden, I be brought up dacent. I know

I wouldn't be in yer league wuth yer class a money or land. I'm prepared ta take a certain amount a shite, but tonight's episode take the biscuit. I is havin nothin more to do wuth your capers, Creeper Madden. I bid you good day.

Where ya headin for, ya madman? Even the dogs in the street knows yer antics, tryin to do a poor auld man and his sister outa their hard-earned few bob, doin their laundry an all – sellin them bags of auld puck turf left out for over a year on the bog an all the kick gone outa it. Not that it ever have any, cause if it done, you'd a burnt it yerself, ya creepy auld monkey-faced bollix. That's it! Run away from me now, ya never could take the heat, ya cowardly auld fecker. That's why ya never get nowhere climbin on the backs of a poor auld helpless pair ridin them all the way to the grave for a few mane lousy bob he have hid under his bed, an I bet you got every dacent note they ever have safely locked in yer own bank vault. Be Jaysus, I know the cure for you! I'll tell Father Mooney!

Be the cuck a Erin, ya shoulda seen the frightened eyes aan him an he flyin past me in the yard, Creeper, says May, his sloppy sister comin intiv the shed. What's all that about goin aan between yis?

Jusht a little bit a lettin him know who's boss, baby dear. Beef an onions on the menu tonight, love?

Bang aan, Creeper.

What's for dessert?

The usual. Me – with or without them aan!

I'll buy you a frilly pair sometime in Daly's when I gather up the nerve.

Jesus, I have to cut much of this for me da or he never let me within a hundert mile of this poisoned farm again, but when it come to Goat I exaggerate it like the divil.

It's back to school a few days later an, lucky for me, Bone forget all about the essay on tin. Sally isn't slow in remindin me tho'. Bringin the ferret inta the class is the day that swing it for me in her eyes, I reckon. The girdles goes crazy when he go dartin about under their desks, but the girdle I have me eye on stay cool as a cucumber. She's no gomey neither, but a fierce bright spark – the auld tech as big a kip for her too.

Like me, Sally have a mind of her own. She don't give a tinker's curse what others think. Of course there's problems in the home with her auld one sozzled a lot of the time on the traipe.

Stay away from that girdle! me granny be warnin.

Why's that? I ask, knowin the answer meself.

Cause she cause ya nothin but hardship.

There's no happiness without a touch a sorrow, I give one of her sayins.

Her father an mother won't want you goin near her.

Her auld man run away to England.

Then her auld one won't want you to be courtin her.

How can you be so sure?

Cause them auld townies an buffers sees hus as dirt.

Sure I's only in trainin. Give me a chance, gran. Isn't every hound a pup til he hunts?

None of that dangerous palaver. A bit of advice tiv you, son. When you goes courtin, leave yer eyes at home, but be sure an bring yer ears.

Our English teacher in the tech is a fat little man wuth a high shiny forehead, an rollin jowls that shudder when he get cross. The reason I mention him at all is cause he read a book wuth hus I love called *Huckleberry Finn*.

Any Traveller worth his salt should take to this book, he tell the class. It's all about a boy called Finn who likes travelling. A good Irish name too. That's why his auld man drinks so much, an in order to have a go at me an Goat the thick caideog says he goes round actin like a tinker, beatin the shite outa his son, Huck. That way he run away from the shams in America an travels down this big river on a raft wuth a black man, meetin all different kind a people. Just like the Travellers does.

You'll never be much good at this subject, Joyce, he say tiv me one day an he handin back me essay. Sure that's the queerest English I read in me whole life. Talk about punctuation goin haywire, to say nothin about your turns of phrase. Where in God's name you got them from beats me. Definitely not Queen's English anyway! There's words here you won't find in no dictionary. You're a quare hawk, Whacker. No chance you mightn't be related to that other puzzler, James Joyce?

Sure me uncle an him's great friends.

I mean the writer, you fool.

No, this man he fix pots, mister. As usual, the class start laughin. I couldn't care less, for Sally's promised to go out wuth me this evenin.

Later she tell me to pick her up at her house. She want to acquaint me to her auld one. Jesus Sally, I is not so sure I want that, I says.

Just like me auld man ushta say – small boats always hug the shore. She's soundin a bit annoyed.

Or one a me auld fella's spakes – a mouse won't win a rat race. Get yer message loud an clear, Sally. See ya tonight then.

She meet me at the dure, gives me a peck on the cheek, an leads me intiv the kitchen. Her mother – thin as a rake, puffin on her last fag, is fidgetin wuth the empty box on the table. Go out and get me ten Craven As, she scowls at Sally. Doin her biddin she give me a wink an a nudge whin she pass, leavin me alone wuth her auld one.

For the few awkward couple a seconds she stare at me, I notice her pair a weary eyes sunk in their sockets wuth black rings round them. Next she start lookin me up an down like I be a animal in some horse fair. This young stallion's not for sale, I feel like sayin.

She don't bear much of a likeness to her daughter at all at all. Standin there in a flowery dress an cardigan – eats like a bird, drinks like a fish – Sally's words come flashin to mind. Seen her before all right – a loner, shoppin in Brady's, or at Mass goin up for Communion. Her face the colour of a block a lard, like that beor that get sucked be a vampire in that filum we see called *The House of Ussher* or some'hin. Then it hit me all of a sudden. She's the mot Bartholomew Brock have wuth him in the pub in Tellamore that Sunday night after Offaly's match in Marboro.

Sit down there an take the weight off the flure, she say at long last, pointin tiv the chair next the table. Wouldn't know how to smile if you tried, I feel like sayin.

Jesus, you is awful quiet, she say then. Did you lose yer tongue or somethin?

To tell the truth, Missus Kelly, I'm a bit shy in yer company.

A bit afraid a me, eh? Hearin stories bout the auld witch, Kelly, an how she do be on the bottle, creatin a scene, is that it? she aks, givin me a flinty look.

To tell the truth, you hit the nail on the head, Missus Kelly.

Who tauld ya all them stories about me?

Some people I hears in the town passin remarks, that's all.

Like who?

I not long enough in the helm to know, Missus Kelly. Well,

there's one, I says then, cause I have a crow to pick wuth the auld bitch.

Well out wuth it, lad.

The Widda Mooney.

That wicked mouthin auld sow. She's so sharp, she'd pick yer bones, an so mane she wouldn't spend Christmas. May a bird outa the sky light on her auld head and pluck her eyes out, the scummy auld witch.

I'm afraid some'hin would want to be done wuth her tongue an ears too, missus. Any'hin bad she have to say about that auld heart scald is music to me ears.

So you've taken a shine to me Sally? she aks me then wuth a frown.

Oh, we help each other in school, an we goes to the odd place together, that's all.

What's bred in the bone, she mutter then. That better be the extent of it young chap, she add, cause if her brothers in England gets to know there's any hanky-panky goin on between ye two, they'll be on the boat in the morning with the crange.

What's a crange, Missus Kelly? I aks in all innocence.

A lad for sniggin yer balls, she say wuth a straight face.

Jesus, is I not glad when I see Sally's head poppin in the dure wuth the witches' fags?

And what you intend doin with yerself, sonny, when you finish school? she aks me, gropin for the packet.

Well, the tin's out, I says. Me da tell me horses or the scrap's the lads for the deener.

An would ya not try your hand at stealin or smugglin? she aks me kinda sarcastic like.

No, I says nice an polite, I prefer to keep on the right side of the law. I'd rather the horses, ma'am, cause very few has the knack a turnin donkeys inta Derby winners.

There's a bit of the knack in you all right, she say rale nasty.

What ya do to earn a crust yerself, Missus Kelly? Sally already tell me, but I is anxious to keep the spotlight away from meself.

Oh, it's a smelly auld job, there's no doubt, makin skins for them sausages outa sheep's gut. There's days you can smell it all over the town. Imagine what it's like inside.

Sure, I says. Pop one on Bart's an you never get pregnant, missus, come intiv me mind then.

Sally – go make yerselfs a cup a tae. I must be off. Make sure there isn't a mess left when I get back, an remember, young Joyce, what I say about Sally's brothers?

Ah, I's a wooden type meself, Missus Kelly.

What you mean?

Wouldn't now nor wouldn't later.

Glad to hear it, Master Joyce.

Out the corner of me eye I sees Sally smilin. I see you get the warnin, she say after her mother leave. Suppose ya know where she's goin?

Out to her boyfriend Bart?

Did she tell you that when I was out gettin the fags?

Not at all.

Then who tell you?

Nobody. I see them together in the pub bout a month ago in Tellamore. So I only guessin.

You're a good guesser.

Her face turn grim then for a few seconds. I know she's gettin ready to say some'hin fierce serious altogether.

I know where I stand in this auld kip, Whack. I'm stuck in

a rut. Me auld fella shags off to England – thanks be to God cause he's no good. Then me brothers follow, leavin me home to be minded by her ladyship, only it's me that's mindin her. I'd love to cut a dash in the big wide world too, only I'm stuck.

Be Jesus you's not, Sally. This fella here bring ya wherever you want. I might be walkin round in a lad's body but I carry a wise nopper on top a me neck. You tell me when, an I'll bring ya tiv any part of the country ya wish.

I'd rather go to England.

Wherever you want. I bring ya.

Then the neighbours be sayin she abandon her poor mother. Who's goin to look after her now they be all aksin.

Sure can't Bart take care of her?

All he want is his bit a nookie. No way two alcos be able to stay under the one roof. A hour or two in the week's as much as he can bear, an so long as she gets her fix, she don't care who she hang out with. When she's got her few drinks, her pride goes out the window. You see me problem?

Ya can't solve yer mother's drinkin for her. It's a doctor or a head shrinker she need after she go off somewhere to dry out, like me auld man when he go intiv the horrors. All you doin is keepin her body an soul together so she can cling to her habit. Someone like that have to hit rock bottom furst. Then you try an claw yer way back.

Easier said than done, Whack. We all know it's time she cried a halt, but she'll not do it on her own or for me. That's why I'm stuck in this auld kip.

Then take the lads in this town. What a shower a stuck-up bollixes most of them is. They'd have nothing to do with a girl from the terraces, specially if her grandparents was Travellers. Oh they wouldn't mind takin me out into the dark night and they blind drunk after shiftin me in the marquee and seein how far they can get. None of them, when they's sober, would ever dream a bringin me home to see their mammies. No, but they wouldn't think twice about making me pregnant and then dumpin me.

Sure never mind them gobshites. What's wrong wuth the other fellas in the terrace, like Alan Murphy or Ger Teevan?

Ah they's goin nowhere. Just like their auld lads on the dole. A shower of dopes actin like they know it all. The last thing they'll ever want is hardship like getting up early and out to work. They'd prefer to stay stuck in this kip an never move.

Well, here's young Jack Joyce, I says, gettin in me spake. Ya won't ketch him on the dole. Never. He a young tinker lad that's keen to get on in the world, an carve out a name an isn't spoilt like a lot a them townies. His mot say he's kinda innocent. Jesus, I not so sure on that. It just that he's kinda awkward in girdles' company.

Well if that's not innocence I don't know what is. Never mind, Whackser Joyce. Is we not a bit young to be settlin?

Give hus a year or two, Sally, when we'll be sixteen. Jesus, how gorgeous you'll look in me arms then wuth hair slides in yer combed back hair, an two big gold hoolahoops hangin from yer cute earlobes, an rakes a gold bangles on yer wristes.

Back to me roots, eh?

Now yer talkin.

Jesus, I don't know if I'd like that. Wouldn't it be a big step backwards, an I wantin to go forward?

But look at what you be gainin? I'm doin me best to convince her. No tax bills, nor rates, go where an as ya please. Sure you be free as a bird.

God, I don't know, Whack. We'll have to see.

I can pictur her missin the shower, the washin machine, the vacuum cleaner. Accordin tiv me da, the greatest curse that ever hit mankind is the ESB.

When I get home, me ma give me a lecture bout goin out wuth a girdle from the helm. But listen ma, I say, Sally's grandparents was Travellers.

But she's not inclined to listen. Well I is on for takin a chance wuth this girdle, I tell her. As me granny say, It's better to be lucky than wise. An look at that Goat's Tail Hussey! He's goin out wuth a townie too.

They'll spell nothin only trouble for ye.

Later that evenin me father bring up the subject wuth me in a vague way too – a sure sign they musta be talkin bout me when I be out wuth Sally. He say tiv me, Son, let me give you this bit of advice. One thing I notice about matches down the years is the ugly's often lucky an the beautiful miserable. Never get too excited bout a pretty face, cause the owner's usually spoilt.

There's nothin spoilt bout Sally Kelly, I says.

Me father's very uncomfortable wuth this subject, I can see by the uneasy glances he's givin me an the jerkin movements of his arms an hands that he's ashamed.

Never mind the pretty puss, he say again. Turn them upside down an they all look the same, son, he say an he headin for the dure.

Lookin back on it, this is the closest he ever get to discussin this matter of the birds an the bees with me, Pecker.

# 19

Out of the blue this Monday mornin we hear a firm knock on our door an we all in bed, each rap of the iron knob sendin a throb thro' me da's hungover head. He come out in his terminal underwear an who's waitin at the step only Grunter, wearin that sleezy grin again – a sure sign he have some'hin else on you – an his sidekick wuth them dead white cheeks hung on his face.

What's ailin ye this hour of the mornin?

We'd like to interview you an your son down in the barracks.

Well we goin nowhere til we's tauld what ye intend to talk to hus about, I speak up for meself.

Look at who's getting cocky now? the Grunter smirks. A chip off the auld block, eh? He sure didn't pick that up off the ground.

Ya goggly-eyed fucker, I mutter under me breath.

Somethin the matter, lad?

Of no interest tiv anyone bar meself.

What exactly's the matter? me da aks then.

Just a little thing a friend want to see ye about that's all.

Our friend can get in touch wuth hus here anytime.

I'm afraid that won't be possible, Mister Joyce.

Why not? I aks.

It's more complicated than that. I can't explain til ye meet me in the barracks.

Who's this friend?

Can't discuss it here. It's too confidential. His sly lurogs glance away from hus.

We discuss this among ourselfs. Sure what have we to lose goin down? me da aks.

He's some'hin up his sleeve, I say, an it smell like a rat.

In the end we agree to go. On our way down me da's mind's racin. Could it have any'hin to do with the O'Brien girdle? he's wonderin. If it is we better stick tiv our main story, son.

Once we is in his little office in the barracks, he plonk his quarter ton arse intiv the seat of the chair behind his desk an stares at hus hard. Someone behind yon door, he say, can prove beyond a doubt that one early evenin in June the pair of ye give a lift to a certain Cora O'Brien an take her all the way to Dublin.

This person's a friend of hus?

Correct, Mister Joyce.

Bring out this so-called friend then, an we'll see what he have to tell tiv our faces.

Next thing our kissers drop when Pork Chops bring out Cora herself. She's lookin horrid – as if she haven't got a dacent night's kip in ages.

I shouldn't have sent that letter, she say tiv hus, her voice breakin.

We both look at each other in amazement. What letter? me da aks.

I sent ye one a fortnight ago from the hotel.

Sure what would they be doin with a letter when neither can read, the sarghint grins.

153

I'm well able, I say, only we don't get no letter.

Then it all come to hus in a flash just like it do to Cora. I bet the guards get their hands on it, she say.

What letter? Garda Fitzmaurice, do we know anythin about a letter?

No, Sarghint Gillick.

That must be how they get the tip off on me whereabouts, she cries, tears rollin. Next thing they come for me in their squad car.

If you must know, pet, we were notified as to your whereabouts by a reliable source in the city of Dublin, says the sarge.

Don't you dare call me a pet! Her temper flashes.

Anyway all that remains is for me to carry out your father's wishes, young girl. He wants to press charges against these two for unlawfully abducting your good self from your place of residence and transporting you to the home of one of their friends in Dublin.

They didn't take me against my will! she cries an we cringin, knowin wuth every word the poor girdle say she's shovin hus deeper an deeper in the mess, an makin the whole scene even more deadly.

That'll be for the judge an jury to decide when ye all have yer day in court, the sarge say. In the meantime I'm required to take statements from you two bucks, so come along wuth me now.

Before we part, me da whisper, Own up to hus givin her a lift to Dublin, nothin further, you hear.

From where?

That bridge down the lane.

What time?

Seven.

When me time come, Grunter try the same trick on me as before, tellin me lies about me da supposin to say this an Cora sayin that.

What you want off me? Me statement or no? I cut him short. When he start writin, I keep what I has to say very short, Pecker. Then he get me to read his writin an aks me to sign it.

After on our way home, me da's in a terrible mood. We get caught cruel bad, Whack. Our little secret's well outa the bag now.

We compare notes. As it happen we more or less say the same things. We see her at the bridge thumbin an give her a lift. She need to get to Dublin an seein we's in no hurry we brings her there. She have no place to stay then, so me da take pity an find her a place at me uncle's for the night.

What make you sure that's what he write?

Jesus, I never think a that.

Did Gillick get you to sign it?

He get me to put a x on the bottom.

But you can't read. He might a wrote any'hin.

Let him. Won't there be fierce fun in court when the judge hear I can't read. I'll say he force me hand.

Still this whole caper have me da fierce worried. Everybody's givin him advice. Bart's sayin he should go see a solicitor, but me da don't trust them lads. They's all in cuckoots wuth one another, he say. An some'hin else, son, don't go near O'Brien's again. Jesus, if you's caught out there we's hung.

I has no intention, I tell him. Course you do, me little voice is sayin inside me head. Can't let auld Birdy away wuth all that cruelty tiv his daughter. Got to help that poor girdle some way. As to how, I hasn't a bull's clue.

An don't be goin round tellin yer buddies about this neither. Clam up if they aks any questions. If you's to say some'hin, tell no more than we say tiv the shadogs.

Yis, boss.

But I'm fierce anxious to hear her version. What she tell the sarge? Is our story much different from hers? Did she tell the whole truth?

That evenin I get fierce restless, an take a stroll intiv the helm. I'm in two minds about what to do til I sees Birdy comin out of Keatin's pub along wuth auld Milly, Cora's fiancé. The thought of them marryin is fit to make me cry more than laugh. They look well oiled too, staggerin down to Lawless's for more of the burly black tack no doubt.

It's getting dark. Go for it, me little voice is screamin. I ramble out of town. Next I'm dashin cross fields huggin the hedges, makin sure I'm not goin to be seen. When I gets near the yard of the cean, I notice his tractor. More than likely he go in Milly's car, or mevvy he's just after gettin back an he's already inside? Thanks be to Jesus he don't manage to get another dog yet, so I sneak over an feel the engine. It's stone cold. I snoop round gawkin in the back windies. Everyhin's dead quiet.

I notice a light in Cora's room. I try the back door but it's locked. I know where he hide the key cause Cora already tell me, so I dash over an fetch it from under the rock. After openin the door, I realise I must leave it back straight away in case Birdy return early.

I open the porch windie, walk out, lock the door from the outside, an leave back the key. Next I crawl back in the windie an close it again. I'm in the act of gettin the key outa the jug for Cora's room when I catch sight of lights flashin outside an before I know it I hear a car pull intiv the yard. I gawk out the windie. Jesus, it's Milly's! I look round in a panic for a place to hide where it be safe. Mevvy the closet? No, he might have some'hin stored in there he want.

I can hear them talkin now on the porch, their mumblin gettin louder. Got to act fast – when me eye catch the settle bed that double up as a bench seat in the corner near the fire. I lift up the lid an slip in – the pong of sour beddin near fit to lift the chuck outa me stomach.

The door open an they come intiv the kitchen. Milly's doin the talkin. Sure ya can't bate a good pair of alsations, Bird. What you say, eh? A couple a right good ones. Sure them two tinkers would never a come near you if them was alive.

Bet they has somethin to do with poisinin them too.

You's dead right about one of hus anyways, I says under the lid.

They'd hardly have the nerve to come back again, would they, Bird? With Gillick keepin a close eye on them an that appearance in court to keep their minds busy, twould take some nerve to return, what, eh?

Better go get another pair quick, or someone might let our butterfly escape.

An where would ya get a few good cheap dogs? Did you try Stacie in the post office? She know all about the different breeds. She keep some grand red setters, herself.

What use is them? Jumpin up on you an slurpin yer face wuth their dribblin tongues, an pissin on yer lap at the same time. All they know is how to make love to ya, Milly Hackett. What use them be for houndin tinkers? Come over near to the fire outa that.

I've no bother hearin what they sayin now with both restin their arses on the lid of the settle bed.

Milly, you'll have a little nightcap fore ya hit the hay.

This frighten the livin daylights outa me underneath. What if Milly intend stayin overnight an usin the settle bed?

There's a little three-quarter bottle of the quare stuff up in the closet. You'll have a sup?

Go home outa that, I'm pleadin.

So she keep tellin ya she want none of the how's yer father when we gets married, Birdy? There's a tinge of disappointment tiv his voice sayin that.

Jesus, you aksed me that already tonight. An what did I tell ya?

She want it wrote in as part of the contract, cause bein a young an tender girl she's makin strange wuth Milly Hackettt, that bony auld fecker wuth his hair in all the wrong places. Sure isn't it only natural.

Well I didn't put it in them exact words. I is too much of a gentleman for that. What else did I say, Milly?

Be patient. Stay calm. She'll get to know me in time. Give her a bit a slack an the barriers drop an in no time she be gaddin round – mad for it.

With who though? I'm thinkin.

What you don't realise, Milly, I got her inta thinkin about this marriage. The only way she'll accept you is with that thing wrote in. Before this, she wouldn't on no account entertain any form of marriage to you. Now she's on for it. Ya get me meanin?

At that he rise an goes over tiv the closet to get the bottle. Let's face up to it, Milly. You is no spring chicken, an definitely no oil paintin. If ya want me daughter you'll have to take her on some of her own terms. Ya get me point?

I can hear him foosterin in the closet. Isn't I lucky I don't hide in there, Pecker.

An is me word not good enough for her? the auld geezer's aksin in a wailin voice. Next thing he let out such a rasper the lid of the settle bed actually vibrate.

You may die of wind comin out both ends of you, Milly Hackett, but you'll never die of wisdom, I says grittin me teeth. None of that better get in where I'm lyin or I be gassed.

That's the trouble wuth them auld hole openers, he complain tiv himself. Bad news eatin them raw, specially fore a session a porter.

What ya groanin on bout now? Birdy snarl at him.

I'm a divil for the raw onions.

Yer stomach linin must be galvanised, he say, handin him the glass. Here's the jug. Pour in yer own measure a water, an he sit down on the bench beside auld Windy Hole. You happy with the arrangement then?

What choice has I? Still I'd prefer she'd take me at me word.

Well to be honest with ya, I'm more concerned that she'll be game for it on the big day fore the priest on the altar. A little more whippin into shape. Don't you worry. I'll have her cutered up for it. To your long health an happiness! I hear him clink his glass agin Windy's. May all yer troubles be little ones, Milly Hackett!

Auld Windy take a slug. Next he let out a little splurtin cough after the sting catch in his wind pipe.

Sure there's a grand lock a soft water in the jug. Here, hauld on til I'll top you up again. This tack's fierce strong.

Next Windy clink his glass agin Birdy's an says, Here's to me new father-in-law to be!

Jesus, don't be rubbin it in. I'm young enough to be yer son.

Jesus, isn't it gas when you think on it?

For you, I says, but that don't include Cora.

Ya sure she be right for the big day then?

Isn't that what I after tellin ya? Anyway what matter if I fail in me efforts. Sure there's pills for every'hin these days.

You mane you might have to make her dopey?

God no. There's a blue pill you can get off yer doctor nowadays that make you happy no matter how sad you feelin inside.

You reckon she be feelin that way then? No touch of love at all in her heart for poor auld Milly?

You know how women is. They gets very highly strung fore a big occasion. One blue fella will rid her of all that. She's only sixteen, remember! How long ago you see that age?

At least fifty, I'm sayin underneath. Seen ya collect the auld age pension last Thursday.

Sweet sixteen! Auld Windy's gigglin out loud now.

Have no fear. I'll deliver from me end. Remember we's talkin bout a lump of no less nor two an a half thousand, an a brand new Ford Anglia. We clear on them issues, Mister Hackett?

God aye, for sure. An no chance of a little peck for Milly fore he leave for home?

Let her lie aisy. She been sulkin a lot lately, specially since returnin from that hotel. Hadn't that tinker some nerve givin her a lift all the way to Dublin, an all the advice I been givin that auld bollix, the Creeper Madden, bout hirin that fella an his young lad. Me tellin him how they'd rob the shite from under you, little realisin they go an rob me own daughter out from under me very nose?

Well you'll get yer own back in court.

Too bloody right we will. Me an the sarge stitch up that Joyce fella. We've a few cards up our sleeves no one know about.

Sure hasn't he a rake a charges again him already? We be makin extra sure they won't be round to try it again.

Proper order for that class a trash. Don't know about you, Birdy, but I'm a man that need me beauty sleep. Seein a little peck is out of order, I better be on me way.

I'm mighty relieved to hear it.

Wait til when she get back to herself. Girls her age is prone to gettin fierce flighty.

Yis, Bird.

By the way, the doctor he prescribe them pills for me the other day.

Did he visit your house or what? Windy sound worried case he might a seen the marks on Cora where he been rabusin her.

God no. I goes in an tell him me nerves is actin up. He make me out a good strong dose. Take it easy, Mister O'Brien, an leave the worryin to others. That's his advice. Be Jesus he a mighty man, Milly. Know what he say last time he visit me for that wheezy chest?

Aye?

If there any'hin that need be done round the farm with yer animals, I'm yer man an I'll do it cheaper an righter nor any vet.

I've heard that about him all right. He's supposed to be mighty talented with his hands.

So I says: Would you be fit to cut a few bulls?

Bob's yer uncle! Next evenin he arrive at the door with the bag an tools. I lead him to the beasts an he get down to business like he at it all his life. He love workin on animals, Milly.

Pure greed's drivin him.

So what if he's savin hus money.

Windy's makin a hard job outa gettin his arse ruz off the bench. I can hear his auld bones creakin. The lid rise a jot when they lift up their bums. Next he let out another ferocious rasper.

Who'd want to sleep next to that? Birdy let out a big guffaw.

I hear their voices fadin down the hallway, while I is lyin there puzzlin what to do next like should I rise an make a run for it when the goin's good? But go where? Soldier it out, the lad in me head's sayin, when in come Bollicky Bill again singin tiv himself:

*Roll me over in the clover an do it again*
*Roll me over in the clover do it again*
*Roll me over*
*In the clover*
*Roll me over in the clover an do it again.*

He sound like he's well sozzled. I lift the lid the tiniest bit an sees him leanin over the bottle a poteen.

Have another nightcap, sir? he say.

Don't mind if I do, Birdy.

You'll have a little water in it, sir?

Proper order, Mister Bird.

He lift up the jug but it's empty. This call for some action, he say, wobblin over tiv the windie next the table, an opens it full. Leavin the jug to one side he hoists himself up restin his tubby belly on the windie board. Then he grab the jug in one hand an lean over to scoop some water outa the rusty barrel outside wuth the downpipe runnin intiv it.

Suddenly this vagary race intiv me head an a rotten wicked one it be too. This bollix is pressin charges again hus. He pushin ahead wuth his daughter's weddin plans again her wishes. She hate his guts.

What if?

I shudder.

Now's yer chance. Up outa that an do it this second! Won't it solve a rake a dacent people's problems? Then duck out the back.

Slowly I lift up the lid, lep out lightly, leavin it open an tip-toe across the kitchen flags. Birdy's head's well sunk in the barrel now, his body leanin an stretchin down so much his fat legs is clean off the floor, grumblin some'hin about the drought leavin the water level too low.

All you need is grab an give them legs a quick sudden lift an his whole trunk slip intiv the barrel so he won't know what hit him. Lights out for Birdy. Do it now! one voice is screamin. If he drown, it's murder! another's naggin me. Suit yerself. You want that on yer conscience? Go ahead.

Think of Cora an yer da! the other one's pleadin. Do it now!

In a flash I grab his stumps an lift with all me might. His tummy slips off the ledge an his whole trunk slide intiv the barrel. Glory be to the divil, but the only noise he make is a low glurg, glurg – his legs stuck up in the air, the boots wrigglin an kickin like crazy, but he can't make a noise no louder than that low glurg. Things is gettin desperate for him now. Leanin his legs again the edge, his whole frame is heavin an shudderin, tryin to topple the barrel on tiv its side, but it's too deep an heavy to manage. The feet's givin up. The water's in his lungs by now surely, squeezin out all the air.

Christ, I gotta get outa here. Nice an easy, Whack. The less you see of this the easier your nightmares. Cora's in her room. Locked. The key's on the dresser. She can't be blamed. Is this the makins of a perfect crime? Ya touch any glasses Whack? No. The porch windie? Yes.

I grab an auld rag off the table. Take one last look at them legs. They is barely wrigglin anymore. Time to skedaddle. Passin the settle bed, I take one last quick gawk in case any'hin drop outa me pockets. Nothin.

I rub the windie well fore slippin through an do the same the other side. I peg the cloth over a wall an I'm out of that yard quick as a whippet, me heart thumpin that mad I can hear it poundin in me ears. The night's warm, wuth plenty a stars sparklin, but thanks be to Christ an His blessed Mother there's no moon. I crawl down long the side of the thick hedge on me hunkers, crossin the road under the bridge an up the bank on the far side, buck-leppin cross thufts of grass in fields, knowin inside me heart an soul what I just do is definitely some'hin you don't win a midal for. I remember what me granny say – Two wrongs don't make a right, sonny – an this hauntin me on the way home. A quiet night in the middle of the week. Feck all stirrin. So far so good. That quare word alibi spring to mind now. Could do wuth a few of them fellas to cover me for that time I'm away. Then they'd want to know what I be up to. When the news break tomorrow they might add one an one an point the finger at me. No, this have to be a pure secret. Sure look what happen wuth Cora? That suppose to be a pure secret too, only it get out. No, I must keep this tiv meself alone. I'm better off doin an sayin nothin.

# 20

When I gets home I notice the light's on in the kitchen. I wait in the turf shed til it go off, which it do round midnight. In the door wuth me an I sneak into bed. I try to sleep but me heart's racin too hard. The minute I shut me eyes, I sees them stumps kickin for all their worth in the air an hear that awful gurgly noise. Let's face it, Whacker Joyce. You just after committin a murder, this rale strict voice inside me's sayin now, an a cold sweat break out on me brow.

Still I manage some kind of uneasy kip. I wake up early when the grizzly episode of the night before hit me again outa the blue wuth a jolt, puttin me intiv the horrors. I hear others gettin up an movin bout the cean, but I lie still – fruze in me bed, too scared to move, or to go to the tilet even.

At round eleven there come a knock on me bedroom door. This is it, I'm sayin, thinkin the worst. Mevvy someone see me leavin Birdy's house last night? Me da come intiv the shady room, the blinds doin a fair good job keepin out the sunlight.

You awake, son?

Just about. I'm bracin meself for the worst.

Birdy O'Brien was found dead this mornin.

You mane a heart attack or some'hin?

Mevvy – it coulda been, tho' they say it look more like a

accident. Leanin out of his windie to fetch some water, he slip intiv his own barrel head furst.

Jesus tonight. What this mean for our case?

He won't be round to press charges.

How's Cora?

Oh he have her locked away in her room as usual, so she couldn't help, tho' they claim she hear nothin.

Who's they?

Neighbours an the shadogs. Sure it's the talk of the town, lad. That what ya get for lyin in bed. By the way, where was you last night?

Jesus, me heart freeze in me chest. Nowhere much, I says, tryin to stay an sound cool.

How come you's in so late?

Got delayed down town wuth the lads.

Hope you wasn't snoopin out near Birdy's?

Wasn't within three mile of it.

Glad to hear. So what you think of the news, eh?

Dunno. What you think?

It couldn't happen tiv a nicer bollix. Get up outa that now. The mornin's nearly over.

I slip out the side of the bed. This mightn't be too bad now? I'm sayin. Still I wonder about a alibi. Me da's aksed me already where I be last night. What if the auld Grunter call me in an aks the same question? This whole episode make me very nervy. It weigh heavy on me mind I can tell you, Pecker.

I can always confess it. All day this debate go on inside me head.

Jesus, Whacker, you look white as a ghost. Is there some'hin wrong with ya? me granny aks.

I not feelin the best. Some'hin in me belly. Still hasn't I me breath which is more you can say bout poor auld Birdy out the road?

Yis. They say the auld traipe done him. They find a near empty bottle a poteen on the table. Auld Milly's suppose to be in a terrible way. Sure waren't they out drinkin together? Hackett carry him home an all. Even went in the kitchen an they has a rake more fore he druve home. Bet the marriage is off now, seein there's no auld fella to hauld the shotgun tiv the poor girdle's head.

Isn't it a funny auld world, granny?

The hand a God work in mysterious ways.

The hand a Whack, gran, I whisper too low for her to hear.

Jesus, I is sayin a fierce load a things under me breath this weather. That's cause I can't tell a livin soul. I think of the cuinnics again. Twould be mad to confess tiv one in this helm. Me mind's runnin riot wuth all the questions me brain's aksin.

Say I goes tiv another helm, a cuinnic he'd want to know when an where it happen. He'd aks me how I murder the geezer. If I tault the truth, I'd have to mention the barrel. How many men dies head down in their own barrels? Surely the cuinnic hear or read about this already on the radio or in the paper?

So what to stop him callin the local sarghint? Tell him some'hin suspicious about that death cause some young fella confess to pushin him in one night an he ought to go investigate it? Seein the late Birdy O'Brien be an outstandin member of the community an a regular Mass-goer, wouldn't they be all the more reasons for callin the shadogs? He not breakin the seal of the confessional cause he not tellin no name? Isn't that right, Pecker?

Or what's to stop him havin a peep at me an I leavin the

box? These cuinnics been known to say one thing an do another. Sure look at Father Rig! Childer is supposed to be safe in the hands of them walkin saints, but look what happen to Noddy? No way can I confess. I'd be takin too many risks. Cuinnics is another type a buffer that can't be trusted.

This secret have me in a terrible mess. Me head's kinda bout to explode. It like a volcano be wellin up inside. Jesus, I must tell someone or some'hin. I think of that story me granny tell me wance bout that king wuth the horse's ears. He tell his secret tiv the trees in the forest an they tell it back tiv his subjects, but I not that big a gomey to believe that. Sure trees don't talk. More like there's someone hidin behind one an hears what the king have to say.

Anyway, this day I take a stroll in the woods outside the helm an come tiv a lovely line a beeches. I take a peep round them, makin sure there's no bollix hidin behind one to hear. No need to holler it out like King Lowry, ya gomey, tho' I know I'd feel a awful lot better if I done. Sure can't you whisper it? Better still, scream it under your breath? Sure it nothin more than make-believe, Whack?

I come tiv the biggest tree in the line. Hello, Mister Beech, I says, an puts me hand out an touch his bark. How I know he's a he? Dunno. Mevvy his size an sheer strength.

You some'hin to tell me, boy? Mister Beech say back.

Yis, boss. I do some'hin cruel naughty lately.

Like?

I kill a auld codger.

That's very naughty indeed! Does anyone else know?

Hope not. That's why I tellin you. You won't pass this on tiv any of me own kind?

No, but I be telling the other trees, if you don't mind.

Includin that auld Down's Syndrome of a bush over yonder?

Look Mister Whack, we's all God's creatures.

Long as none of them pass it on, like ye do tiv poor auld King Lowry?

You mean the gomey wuth the horse's ears?

Now you talkin, Mister Beech.

That's only a fairy tale. More serious now. Why you kill this gom? Was it in self-defence?

No, Mister Beech.

Then it not just a killing. This sound more like murder.

Yis, boss. That why I'm here.

This sort a banter go on for ages. Me tellin the tree an he talkin back. All takin part in me own head, Pecker. That's how desperate I am. When I leave the wood, I feel a lot better cause I know some'hin that live hear me secret.

A few days pass wuth no news. The fact that Cora's locked up again her will in her room an her showin the marks of him rabusin her have a load of people showin sympathy for her. Next she squeal bout that auld goat Milly wantin to marry her in return for a big lump a money an a brand new car. This have many tongues waggin.

Then Milly himself's forced to confess tiv the arrangement, as well as admittin they be both mouldy drunk on the night of the tragedy, along wuth the fact there's no sign of any intruder. These all makes it a closed an shut case. A tragic accident, Pecker.

This is the way me mind's spinnin – gettin more cocky by the day – til one mornin I'm strollin by the barracks wuth nothin on me mind when the Grunter poke his snout out the door an say, Could you spare me a few minutes?

What for? I aks, me heart jumpin intiv me mouth.

Just a few routine questions.

Concernin what?

That accident out in O'Brien's.

What of it?

Seeing you been snooping out there before, I'd like to ask you a few questions.

Believin the best form a defence is attack – I'm havin no more of yer trick questions, Sarghint, I shout in his face, tryin to cod me into admittin tiv false information before. You ought to be thrun out of the guards.

Where were you the night of the tragedy, Master Joyce?

What you goin to accuse me of next? I be seen in O'Brien's. Is that it?

I asked a simple question. Where were you on that night?

Why don't you get the auld judge to aks me that on the day of our case?

You'd have a strong motive, you know?

What do you mean? The smart ass use a word I don't understand.

A man brings a serious case against you. Is that not a strong reason for doing away with him? That's what that means, young fox.

You thinks I'm a animal you can hunt?

The way he's starin, the bollix is lookin for signs a weakness in me, but thanks be to the divil, that chat I have with the tree do me a world a good. I even get a few good nights' sleep out of it. By this stage me panic's festerin intiv a raw hate an I'm enjoyin me little tiff wuth the Grunter, specially now that the townies passin the door is all ears. All the more embarrassin for Grunter than me, seein we's suppose to have no pride. I can act the tinker wuth the best in the helm cause that what's expected.

You reckon I'm a wild animal you can hunt? I shout wuth all me might, when I spies the lanky Monsignor comin our way in his long black cassocks an sharp baldy head.

Are we havin a little problem here? he aks the sarge. The auld gomey pull in his horns now in a hurry, Pecker.

He sayin he'll hunt me down like a fox, Father, an he try to put words in me mouth, accusin me of doin things to the poor late Birdy when I nowhere near the place. There's no justice in the world for the likes a hus, Father. I'm tryin me best hand at cryin.

I succeed pretty well too – puttin on quite a show for them auld women gawkin. This story she'll travel now an the more ashamed that auld sarge look the more me tears is fallin. He have no choice but to back away from his attack.

These things really ought to be discussed in private – not in the middle of a public thoroughfare, Sergeant, do you not think?

I'm still puttin on a great show a crocodile weepin.

Get away with yourself, now, you trouble-maker! Grunter shout.

But I refuse to stir. I'll go when you give me an apology, Sarghint Gillick.

Apology for what?

Callin me a wild animal, an accusin me of doin things I knows nothin about!

Get away with yerself now, and not be disturbing the peace or I'll lock you in the cell!

Next thing Joe Joe appear outa the crowd. Come with me son, he say. We all know you been getting a raw dayle from that fella ever since ye come into the town. Picking on the poor and helpless rather than the real criminals – a real sign of a bully that, isn't it, Monsignor? Come on, Jack, I'll walk you home, an we stroll away rale brazen like, the crowd nearly fit to cheer.

We's no sooner off the main street when Joey say, Time we made another telephone call. Let's play another trick on them bullies.

From the telephone box he call the barracks an get Pork Chops on the other end. Joey's a fierce man for the accents. What he use now is a total different one to what he use lasht time. Hello, Guard. Hope you don't mind me callin for a bit of information concernin me son. He's fierce eager to join the force, but the lad's an inch short of the regulation height.

What size is his shirt collar?

Sixteen.

What's his waist width?

Thirty-six inches, Guard.

Jesus, he'll have no problem then.

One other thing.

Yis?

He's after doin his Group Cert an …

He passed it?

No bother.

Then what's yer problem?

I'm worried he might be a bit over-educated like for the job. What's your opinion on that, Guard?

Who the hell are you anyway? Where ya callin from?

Joe Joe slams down the phone.

Jesus Joey, I say, how you keep a straight face thro' all that's beyant me.

*

The story about me run-in wuth the Grunter travel all over the place. They all talkin bout the way the Monsignor stand up to Gillick like that over the way he treat a travellin lad. Me da have a bag a questions when I gets home.

How all that start, son? he want to know.

He say he'd run me down like a fox.

You start bawlin on account a that?

I only puttin on a act, da.

Rale tears flowin in bucketloads?

Who tell you that?

Sure there's scores a witnesses. What else he say tiv you?

I stay silent.

There have to be more to this than meets the eye. Remember me tellin you before, son, you can come clean with me, cause I never let you down. I protect you no matter what – thro' thick or thin. No matter how wrong the thing you do, your secret's safe wuth me. Is there some'hin else he accuse you of?

I'm still not sure if I should tell. He gettin ready to accuse me of bein out in O'Brien's on the night.

Was you in his house that night?

I already tauld you no.

He's starin me hard, like he can see thro' intiv me heart where that big dirty secret's locked away.

I is aksin for the truth, son, any'hin less is a lie.

Betimes they may be necessary.

That may be, but in this instance any'hin less than the truth will not do. I'm aksin all these questions to protect you. No matter how bad all this is, get it out of yer system, that's all I tryin to do.

Be Jesus, Pecker, it all pour out of me like red hot lava. Me secret's shared. Me da he listen wuth not a budge out of him.

A temptin situation I'll admit, he say after a long silence, an
you know, Whack, if I war in your place I'd a done the very
same. That won't help you out of yer misery, I know, cause you's
the one that done the deed, but I'll do me best to get you thro'.
This is one thing that must remain a secret from everyone, an
that include your mother, granny, sister, brothers, uncles, aunts.
I not goin to whisper this tiv anyone. Twould be deadly if it get
out. Birdy's gone an can't be brought back. No loss neither.
Cora don't know no better herself. Don't let it get tiv you, son.
Look what happen in all them wars – people shootin or stickin
bayonets intiv each other an not a word about it. We fight our
own little war wuth that frigger on the half of his rabused
daughter. So long she not know what happen, she not know
any better. This case be wrote off as a accident. Gillick love to
pin it on someone, right or wrong, so he can get a permotion.
That why he's so deadly. Mevvy at last people's beginnin to see
thro' him. Son, remember this. Your secret's safe wuth me.
Where you be the night that happen?

Out in Birdy's house.

No. You war in the van wuth yer father. That's all you have
to say if he ever aks you again.

Goin where?

Checkin out a few nags off a Traveller in Arklone.

# 21

One evenin a week later Ribleen come to me wuth a message from Noddy. He want me an Goat to meet him later that night in the same place as before. I'm walkin round wuth a lighter gimp now after I pour out all that dirty secret tiv me da. Even them nightmares goes away, an I'm sleepin a lot better.

When I leave to go out of the cean, me da plant a word in me ear. Remember not a word to Goat nor Noddy, you hear?

Better nor a garden angel you is, I says.

Me an Goat arrive on time at the hide, wonderin what it's all about. Noddy's late as usual. About ten minutes later he step in wuth a big wide grin on him from ear to ear. Suppose ye know why we's here?

Me an Goat looks at each other. We hasn't a clue.

It's nearly two month now since we last meet an I'm most surprised ye can't remember, specially seein it your suggestion, Whack.

Ya mane Stacie's pups?

She go out this mornin expectin to see a litter of the finest thoroughbreds – a waitin list of twenty clients tearin at each other's throats for one of her prized dogs – an what she find? Nine of the ugliest-lookin mongrels you could clamp eyes on, an eight of them bitches! How could this happen? she's squealin. Slattery tell hus all in the hotel today at lunch time, an she blamin him. Great idea, Whack. Well done. It work to perfection. Last but not least, I wish to thank that horrid-lookin mongrel who play no small part in the adventure. Now for our next trick. My turn this time. You's goin to love me choice. Any idea who it goin to be, fellas?

Me an Goat just shrug.

How about our big soft cuddly sarghint?

Jesus, he's far too dangerous to hit, Goat say.

I've the tastiest little prank ye ever imagine.

What might that be? Goat aks.

That's a little secret.

Hope you is not involvin me after what I be thro' wuth that bollix? I says.

Me word of honour, Whack. It don't affect you at all. Finally, would any of ye be interested in a part-time job in the hotel at the weekends? Me boss ask me to look round for someone to help in the kitchen.

I too busy helpin in the chip van, Goat tell him.

Would you be interested, Whack?

I'll try any'hin, I say, knowin it help keep me mind off that other racket.

Twill be worth a nice few bob too – one of the good things of bein a member of the Pavee Club.

What ya have in mind for Grunter? Goat aks.

Let me worry bout him. Ye'll love this prank, lads.

The followin evenin I meet Noddy outside the front door of the hotel. He bring me in an introduce me to Billy, the chef, a small round butty man wuth a greasy face an glazed eyes from all the red wine he's sneakin. He get kicked out of a posh hotel in Dublin an the boss snatch him up.

I'm meant to keep the kitchen tidy, like sweepin the floor

clean, washin dishes, or poppin down tiv the cellar to fetch up some peck outa the big fridge when needed. At the end of the night I'm expected to wheel out all the heavy bins a trash, that why they want a strong fella like me.

Before Noddy go out to wait on the tables, he take me to one side. Guess who's comin to dinner at nine?

Grunter of course.

How ya ever guess?

Hope you don't intend poisonin him?

Could easy happen.

Durin the next few hours I'm left wonderin what Noddy have up his sleeve.

At nine on the stroke he dash in. One porterhouse medium-rare an one baked sole, he call.

I get sent tiv the cellar to fetch the steak. Noddy follow me down. You want to see the get-up of the pair of them in the dinin room, Whack. He's dressed rale fancy like in a black suit an flashy tie. She's in a black spangly dress wuth a low neckline that show off a fair bulge a freckly tit, an she wearin loads a sparklin jewellery. Beyond doubt they regard theirselfs as big nobs. Any night they's in, they walk out after eatin without ever payin. Some arrangement between him an the boss in return for keepin the bar open long as he like.

Noddy open the fridge an pull out this lovely glistenin slab a beef. Next he peg it up at the ceilin. It hit it flat on wuth a slap swattin a fat bluebottle takin a rest from his buzzin. For the shortest length it stick fore peelin off an fall back down. None of hus makes any attempt to catch it fore hittin the floor. Noddy bend down an pick up the steak an places it on the butcher block table. Now, Whack, I want you to witness this.

In a flash he loosen his belt, slip his trousers down an cock up his bum, grab the meat, give his arse a good wipe wuth it fore slappin it on the tray, then pullin them back up he straighten himself. This one steak that won't need seasonin, Whack.

I run back with the meat on a tray to Billy who throws it into the waitin pan. In no time Noddy's placin it under Grunter's gob. I'm peepin out thro' the hatch hole, his bulgy eyes feastin on the sizzlin steak, big pink bib tucked in at the shirt collar, elbows risin together, knife in one hand, fork in the other and down they dive to attack the meat. I see the furst lump enter his mouth. He's chewin. How's your steak, Sarge? I'm lip readin Noddy now.

Delicious! he's beamin. He tell me it have a beautiful flavour, Noddy say later. Goat nearly get sick wuth the laughin when I tell him what happen.

*

All that be great fun at the time, Pecker, but jusht to show ya how dangerous this Grunter fella is – Joe Joe tell me he hear some shams in the helm say he very angry over me makin little of him in front of the Monsignor, an he intend gettin his own back on hus.

This evenin there's money took out of a house in the town. Me da's wobblin home later that night. He carryin a load a garaid he get outa doing a dayle, selling a lock a mountain goat he pass off as deer tiv a cakesham in the gat cean.

Next thing the squad car pull up beside him. Grunter lower the windie. He want to know where he comin from. Me da get stubborn cause he have a good streagale a skyhope in him. Grunter an this other shadog – they jump out an pin him tiv the wall. Grunter search his jacket pockets an come upon the pile a deener. He then try an blame the robbery on him.

Sure we all know he carry a chip on his shaulder, Pecker.

They take him in tiv the barracks. Course he don't want to tell the shadogs where he get the money cause he after doin a swingle.

A case a bein in the wrong place at the wrong time, Pecker. They keen to pin it on somebody an what better man than Jim Blocker Joyce! Again, the shadog aks him where he get the deener. He refuse to say. The Grunter then come on the scene wuth his big black dildo.

Where else would the likes a you get so much money exceptin ya stole it? he accuse him.

I be mindin it for another man, me da say.

Who's he?

None of yer business.

Again he corrip the lard outa me father. It get so bad, the other shadog have to pull the black caideog off him for fear he might kill him altogether.

He still refuse to tell.

Next Grunter write up a statement for me da to sign but he refuse. Next he grab his hand an try to force him scribble a X. There's a mighty scramble an a mark get scrawled right across the page. Ya rotten tinker, Grunter holler. You just after ruinin a perfectly good confession. You know what this mean? Another mighty skelpin for you.

Himself an another shadog then beat him round the room.

Grunter write out another quare confession.

Now sign yer X to this fore I kick yer teeth down yer throat. Me da's mouth's already bleedin an he in a very weak state after all that corripin, so when Gillick grab his hand to force him to sign, me da let out a huge bloody spit on tiv the paper.

Jesus, the sarge shrieks, grabbin his hair an forcin his head down. There, you smelly bastard, lap that up wuth yer tongue fore I choke ya.

He get cruel horrid treatment at the hands of the Grunter Gillick on this occasion. Again, he get yet another summons to appear at the next sittin. Jesus, Pecker, by this stage all the charges agin him's really pilin up.

# 22

One grand fine September day me an Eyebrowser goes ramblin down by the river longside Hennessy's egg farm to the place where Teevan get the fright of his life wuth the rat. No doubt but the spot's still teemin wuth them an Eyebrowser's doin fierce sniffin an growlin. Jesus, me, Noddy an Goat we musht have a go at them barborious big rats again here fierce soon, I is sayin tiv me dog, when who pop outa the bushes only the Hennessy buffer himself, burly an broad wuth a red phizog on him an a heavy Offaly jaw an a head a wiry hair like a lectric current's goin thro' it.

Howdy stranger, he say, talkin like a cowboy. Ain't seen you round these here parts. You new to the town or what?

We's moved in a few month.

Up in the terrace?

Yis, boss.

You're one a them Travellin families so?

We is.

It's hardly me eggs you're after?

I'm on the wrong side of the bank for them, mister.

You know about them then?

I come to admire yer rats, boss.

Suppose you know why it's alive with the little buggers?

Yer hen shit an feed?

They's gobblin me feed an eggs be the new time all right but they leavin the other stuff. If I'd ever me way again I'd never a built them sheds so near that fuckin river. Seem a good idea first with the water close for washin, cleanin, an wettin d'auld mash.

Rat poison's yer only man for them auld nests, mister.

They's even taken to borin holes in me eggs an suckin out the yolks, but divil a shite I care. Hasn't I loads a fat weanlin lambs an suckler ewes? Sure hens is only a hobby. I even see one fella last week – a brown hoor brazen as you like – an he rollin one of them long the path with his sniffer, headin for the river there.

Rat tak's yer only man for them lads, boss.

Works for a while. Next thing fore ya know it they's back strong as ever.

You want to keep it well planted, mister. Keep a few good terriers round the place too an mevvy a few creepers.

Creepers?

Cats, mister.

Bet you won't believe it when I tell ya this. Them rats is the least of me worries. Granted we is losin feed an eggs be the new time an I hates the livin sight of the little feckers, but at least they leave the hens alone. You know what's me biggest scourge?

Foxes?

Be Jesus there's no flies on you. Who tell ya that?

Sure what else would trouble chickens apart from a stray dog or some'hin?

You know much about them?

Yis, boss.

One she-fox has me heart scalded an some bitch of a vixen she is at that. Comes in the dead of night. The shit's so scared outa the hens, they find it hard to lay even when she don't come. We often lie up all night with guns waitin but she smell us a mile away.

Ya ever try layin poison round the sheds instead like in a dead hen?

Tried everythin. Even the best fox-hunters in the parish track the bitch but they never manage to catch her. Sure they trace her a mile or two. Then the trail disappear into thin air.

He point across at this huge stretch of scrub, sand hills an bogland. You'd walk ten mile any way in that an never see a single house. Somewhere out there that where she's hidin.

It's well I know the ground, Pecker. Sure I trace the river flowin thro' it one time. Would ya not keep a few dogs tied up round the sheds, mister?

And have them up all night barkin at their own shadows, rousin the dead an frightenin the shite outa me hens, stoppin them from layin even worser?

Ya ever try snares or a few traps?

Try everythin. She avoid them like the plague. Last week she get into one of me sheds – kill dozens just for the sheer fun. Then she take a few nice plump ones.

The furst thoughts comin intiv me nopper then – if she's cartin some of the hens, she can't be livin too far away. Failin that she storin them someplace where it's cold an safe, like them townies wuth their fridges. Course I too cute to tell him all that, Pecker.

An ye follow her trail? I aks him instead.

Only so far. Then it disappear.

She know how to use the river, I says tiv meself. While I'm thinkin this over, yer man's busy makin up a trick question to catch me out.

How you know we know she's a she?

Her shit, pee an paw marks. Why?

Be Jesus you're well up. How you know the men knew she act on her own?

Paw marks would tell them that.

You know your onions, lad, there's no doubt. You hunted foxes before?

Me an me uncle often raid their dens an takes the cubs to rear or for cross breedin. He's big inta dogs.

What's his name?

The Puckeen Hussey.

Can't say we ever met. An yerself?

They call me Whacker Joyce, boss.

Any chance ye might try yer hands at catchin this scourge?

Well we give it a try anaways.

Bring her to me dead or alive an I'll give ye thirty pound, you hear?

Spot on, Mister Hennessy.

Back home I tells me uncle every'hin bout the fox – bar the reward he's givin. I'm hopin to collect that for meself so me an Sally can go on a bit of a tear.

That fox is no fool, Whack. Bet she get trapped before an learn the hard way. Only I is too busy I'd lep tiv the challenge. Take me best fox terrier – yerself an Goat – an give him a sniff round Hennessy's sheds furst. If ye draw a blank, come back tiv me an mevvy some Sunday we all have a gander together.

When I goes lookin for Goat, he's busy helpin a farmer out the road wuth the corn, so I hop down an aks Sally. She's very doubtful about this whole caper at furst but seein the grand day that's in it she's easily persuaded.

I take her down by the river on our piebald pony. She's not too sure of her bearins at furst on the nag's back but she come to terms wuth him quite fast an I leadin them wuth the reins.

We make our way down to Hennessy's hen sheds. The fox's scent is faint enough. Still he pick it up an we follow him intiv the brush.

We is headin intiv a different world. I see it wrote in Sally's gleamin eyes any time I glance back. When she get confident enough, I leap up behind her, hauldin the reins, an we gallop together down the path til the horse stop on top of a strong hill. What a view we both see on that misty day! Birch ash an beech below hus an the river snakin her way ripplin over baulders, the Puckeen's favourite fox terrier standin proud close beside, his tongue pantin, his feather-tail cocked.

Her long flowin blond hair's fornenst me. Jesus, an me dyin to nibble at her nape, her firm back an curvy bottom in her denim jeans me heart pumpin like crazy an I sayin tiv meself there an then I'll go to any end fair or foul – fight tiv the death – to be marrit tiv this beor. Sure you already sell your soul to the divil on account a Birdy O'Brien. Why not enjoy the rest of your life on this earth best you can, you randy little get? As me granny say, You sow the wind, ya might as well reap the whirlwind.

If we's the Injuns as you be sayin, Sally, then you's me squaw, I says in her ear, an she let a whoop outa her that startle the pony an annoy the dog cause he's just after pickin up her trail again.

An have you a good squaw name for me?

Sure. That monicker I see in the pictur wance bout Peter Pan in the Savoy. How about Tinkerbelle?

Who you'll hauld ontiv til death squeeze out me last breath if it's not squeezed out of you first?

Whin will we jump the budget?

What you mean?

Just a sayin me granny have bout gettin marrit.

Sure you're only a scut.

You be very surprised on that score, Sally Kelly.

What's your age then?

Getting up there. I knows lots a Travellers long marrit at my age.

Whack, you're some dreamer.

The hound stop at the edge of the river. He's run outa scent.

This is where the vixen get clever, Sally. She have the knack a usin the water to bate the hunters.

An who'd blame her? Isn't they supposin to be clever? So what if she nab a few hens? Maybe she's a family to feed. I'll bet she need them more than that Hennessy frigger. What that bollix ever do for anyone? If I was you, I'd leave that poor auld fox alone.

If she's that clever, the chances is her cubs is very smart too an with a bit a luck we breed some of that cuteness intiv some class a dog if we can get them both to mate. You get me meanin?

So long as you wouldn't be harmin them, that's all I is sayin.

Harmin or no harmin we's goin to have some job findin her furst. What we goin to do now that we's come tiv the end of the trail, Tinkerbelle?

Your uncle shoulda give you two hounds – one for each side of the river.

I give her a hug from behind.

Know why I don't think a that?

Why?

Your scent have me all confused.

Go aisy or we'll both fall in the river.

Might cool me down, I is sayin tiv meself, jumpin off the pony an followin the hound to the river edge.

The only way we can manage this, I tell her, is we go a length up one side. If he don't pick her up there, we may cross the stream an come back down long the other edge.

What if he picks up the wrong trail?

He won't. The great thing bout this fella he can hault the one scent. Send him after that one, he follow that one.

Amazin.

The Puckeen train it intiv him. That's why he special.

So we follow the dog on our side of the river. About a half mile up we happen to be lucky – or so we think. The dog pick up the she-fox trail again an he lead hus thro' high bog wuth the heather coverin a sod firm enough for the pony's hooves not to sink. However the trail it wind back tiv the river an disappear again.

She's leadin hus on a wild goose chase, Sally says.

Still the point we's at jog me memory, Pecker, for I happen to remember a quarry that's situated kinda close by. Mightn't she be usin some part of this for storin her hens, say among rocks where it's dark an cold, I'm wonderin? The dog's sniffin the air for a sign but there's none.

So we push on for the quarry an sure enough the hound get the scent again in among the baulders. He find it rale strong this time, an on a stone slab we come on a rake a chicken feathers. The ground's too shingly for the pony, so we follow the dog in a line outa the quarry an fornenst hus is undergrowth so thick only the hound can go in. This could be where she's livin, I says, til we hear him whimperin inside more outa flustration than excitement.

Don't tell me he's lost her again?

There's no flies on this fox, Sally Kelly.

By this stage the sun's sinkin below the dark rock wall face of the quarry. The time's passin.

I'm getting mighty hungry, Sally says, readin me own mind too. She bring a lock a sandwiches, a can opener for the tin a beans she take, as well as a spoon for eatin them.

You is a mighty girdle, I say, helpin her to spread the peck out on a flat slab near tiv the fox's table where she leave the tell-tale feathers. I drag over two rocks for seats an we tear intiv the sandwiches. As she bends over me, I catch a glimpse down the front of her loose-fittin blouse. Her buddin breasts so lovely an firm wuth no bra on. Smooth salla skin tight all the way down past her belly button just bout ingrown. The place where we sit have the sun all day til now an leave the rocky ground nice an warm, a light breeze carryin a whiff a mouldy moss off the limestone slabs.

When I finish eatin, I lies back on the mossy ground, starin up at the dark blue yonder an say, Isn't the sky up a cruel depth today, Tinkerbelle?

Millions a miles deep, Whack.

Jesus, she's much deeper nor that.

How you know?

We gettin out of our depth now.

No end tiv it I suppose?

Endless is hard to dig, Sally.

Like shapeless or timeless. Can I give you a kiss, Whack?

She lean toward me an, grippin me face in her hands, kisses me hard an wet on the mouth. A lovely smell an taste like milk on her baby-warm breath. Next thing she's lyin next me starin intiv me lurogs, mesmerisin them til I'm forced to look away.

She start grindin her crotch hard again mine then – me kneedin her butt cheeks wuth me fingers. A force surgin inside me body like a fever. She's slippin her hand down between me legs now, me lovin the way she's makin all the moves. Fore we know it we's tearin like mad at our clothes pullin them off hus like we invaded by pissmires or some'hin.

Jesus, I feel like a king, a voice inside me's braggin.

King of what? another one's aksin.

Thrills, me biy! One day you're a bloody murderer pure an plain – another day you is losin yer cherry. What'll tomorrow's thrill be, Whackser?

Jesus, I can't wait, I'm cryin, an she fondlin me mutton soldier. An you know what, Pecker? When we doin it, I gets this funny notion the she-fox's watchin hus thro' the bushes. The prettiest little beor in the whole animal kingdom! Sure isn't it tome for a nobody like me for to be turnin the likes a her on. A mighty boost, biy, an hus pleasurin each other. You get me meanin?

This thrill's so strong, I know I won't last much longer when guess who come tiv me rescue? None other than the bauld Birdy himself. The ghastly puss of him flash intiv me head. There's that fuckin barrel again, only it have a glass bothom tiv it this time round. I'm lyin underneath it gawkin up at this desparate pair a bulgin eyes, his snortin nose nudgin again the glass, the mouth sucked in starved of air – about to cave in tiv the water.

A horrid pictur to be comin between me an our love-makin. It certainly put a bit of a halt tiv me gallop, which without her knowin it, turn out to be grist for Sally's mill. Birdy's strangled stare stop me from comin ahead a her.

Am I right in the head at all I'm wonderin while she's

189

wringin out her last little shudders an groans from deep down in the animal end in her.

That's how life begin, I hiss in her ear, when all our ripples dies away.

It better not, Sally shoot back.

Yer furst time?

No, nor me second. How bout yerself?

Never til this minute.

Get outa that. I don't believe ya!

I tellin no word of a lie.

I mean the way you handle all that. You'd swear you's doin it every night. For a young scut, you got great stayin power, Whack. There's no contest between you an me other lads.

Who's they?

That's a secret.

I catch a naughty gleam in her eye. Jesus, you is some cookie, Sally Kelly. You know some'hin?

What?

While we is doin it, don't I see the fox starin at hus outa the bushes an a great smile on her gob.

You not serious?

Me eyes is finer tuned nor any buffer's.

So's yer ears.

I'd love to live out here wuth all the wild animals. Wouldn't it be great?

If the weather hold like this all the time, an we've plenty a tinned food an a washin machine an a roof over our heads. All the things a lad like you wouldn't ever dream a havin. Tell me you ever stop dreamin?

I have the odd nightmare too.

Is there any'hin botherin you, Whack? Somethin's come intiv ya lately, hasn't it?

When?

In the last couple a weeks.

Just a little tired that's all, I says, angry at her cuteness in bein able to cop me on so well.

Now that the chill of the evenin give hus goose pimples, we slips intiv our clothes. The evenin's closin in an we be a good few miles from the helm. We mount the pony an head for home again, leavin the she-fox for another day.

Three days later Hennessy catch sight of me in the street. She strike again last night, he say wuth a long glum puss on him.

How many?

She mow down ten.

Have her for ya by Monday.

Heard that one before. Did ye try trackin her yet?

We be out there a few days ago.

Have any luck?

Nothin more than a biteen a wool, I says smilin.

You mean she's attackin sheep as well?

Could be.

What makes you so cocky you'll get her fore Monday?

We a fair idea where she's lyin.

That afternoon I'm upstairs in the attic haulin a few good fox traps out of the heap a junk. Oilin them up good an proper I is up on me pony – alone this time, apart from the Puckeen's hound – settin out on the trail again after givin him another sniff of the fox round the sheds. This time the scent's good an strong.

After about a hour I'm in the quarry an set bout buryin the

traps along the trails where the hound find the smell is strongest.

Next mornin I'm up bright an early an on me pony headin for the quarry, not too sure what to expect – certainly not to find the six traps dug up an all snapped tight. The cute bitch set them off by pokin sticks intiv each one, which she musta hauld in her mouth. Sure what else way could she snap them, Pecker?

This is some cute fox, the Puckeen tell me the minute I give him the story. This is a sure case for the magic liquid, he say, an one thing, Whack, don't for the life of you bring any more traps. She allergic tiv them. Go find a natural hole somewhere near tiv the quarry. On no account you try an dig one out. You hear?

Why's that?

Cause she'll get the whiff a fresh clay an smell a rat.

He go away an come back with a small dark-brown-coloured bottle. You ever smell this stuff? he aks me.

Never. I pop the little cork an put it tiv me nostrils.

Yuk, I says after takin a sniff. That'd turn yer stomach.

Love potion for a she-fox, says Puck, an he tell me how to use it.

Saturday mornin I'm off on me own this time without dog or pony. I scour round for a good deep hole as the Puck say. Sure enough I find one close tiv the quarry. It seem like it be dug by the men who work there many year ago. For what reason I'm not rightly sure.

It take me a time gatherin greesha, leaves an moss. The whole job's to make it look natural an I has to be extra careful on that score, Pecker. I take a rock an place it right on the edge, sprinklin some love juice on the side facin the covered hole, an hope for the best.

Next mornin I'm up at the crack a dawn, sneakin me way out toward the quarry. Fore I know it I is standin over the rock starin down at the vixen rolled in a ball in the bothom of the hole. Horny auld bitch, I sneer at her.

She make one more desperate lep to try an get herself out but she don't even reach halfway. There's nothin for it but for me to race back home an get me some rope an the wire cage the Puckeen use for trappin foxes an badgers cause I intend keepin me word to Sally bout bringin in the she-fox alive. Sure, hasn't I already kilt enough varmin in me life?

Sally, I've news for you, an I meetin her in the terrace on me way back home.

You kill that poor fox?

No but I ketch her.

Suppose you goin to kill her later?

If I goin to do that, I'd not be here talkin wuth ya now.

Did anyone ever tell you you isa very unusual fellow?

Far as I know, I just be like anyone else.

Well you isn't, Whack Joyce. What's yer plans for that poor auld fox then?

I intend bringin her tiv Hennessy in a cage, gettin me reward an then releasin her up in the Slieve Blooms.

What if Hennessy say – How's we to know that's her, sure that could be any auld fox you ketch – an refuse to give ya the money?

The proof of the puddin's in the eatin. It depend how many more hens gets narked. Anyways, we'll cross that bridge when we gets tiv it.

# 23

Me da make Creeper a promise we be out tiv him first thing Monday mornin to help wuth the pratie pickin. I is kinda lookin forward to a break from school cause it gettin on me wick again.

Sunday evenin I goes out wuth Goat an together we cage the fox an brings her home. Any'hin like the ructions the dogs makes an we puttin her in the shed 'twould waken the dead, Pecker.

That night when me father don't return home, nobody's terribly put out cause he does this many's the time without warnin beforehand. We make a hunch he meet up wuth Bart somewhere an they start drinkin, which they often do before, but when I hear this loud knock on our door late the followin mornin, I don't like that one little bit. It spell out that maybe some'hin's wrong. Then to be met be a strange shadog, well that send shivers up me spine, Pecker.

Me ma come tiv the door then too an I can tell by the look on her face that she suspect some'hin bad happen. What the shadog tell on the step well none of hus is ready for this. He say they have to keep me da overnight in the barracks an when they come tiv him this mornin, they find him unconscious in his cell.

Where's he now? I aks.

In the hospital.

Can we go see him?

I'm afraid not.

Why's that?

Maybe later. This young shadog's gropin for words.

Me ma cop it right away. What part of the hospical is he in?

The morgue.

Jesus, we don't know what hit hus, Pecker. Nothin's more final than death. As me granny say, The man at sea may return but not the man in the graveyard, an me more knowledged about that nor anyone five times me age at the minute. We'll never see me auld da alive again.

Me ma break down, while I stand there grittin me teeth. This hit me so fast it numb me senses. I do me best to gather meself.

I aks the shadog, How come you's comin so late wuth this news?

He'd to be rushed into hospital first for to find out what kill him.

What he die of?

A brain haemorrhage.

What bring that on?

Dunno, lad.

There's a uneasy silence. I'm sorry for your troubles, folks, he say then, bowin his head a little an touchin the shiny peak of his navy cap, fore turnin on his heels an headin back tiv his thick buddy waitin in the drivin seat of the squad car.

There's too many unanswered questions here, I says. Why they take him in last night? Did they arrest him or what? Was he beat? Why the strange shadogs? Where's the Grunter?

Gone from hus forever, me ma's wailin, an he only forty-six.

Me granny come on the scene an then Ribleen an now there's almighty keenin. No more yarns nor jokes. Who will I go to now for advice an support? These things racin thro' me nopper. Me dark secret – he bring that wuth him too.

The Puckeen an Molly come out tiv hus. I could feel it for months in the auld crystal ball that some'hin awful goin to happen, Molly say, but twouldn't give me no name, an I wonderin if it mightn't be meself. Instead it's poor auld Blocker, who wouldn't even harm a fly.

The time seem to freeze. We just sit round not knowin what to do. There's fierce sobbin an wailin outa the women. Unbeknown to hus, the word's spreadin rapid on the bush telegraph, thanks tiv the Widda Mooney an Stacie Williams. I'm too numb to think straigh or to feel any'hin like the anger that grip me later. That how it go when you tryin to come to terms wuth a loss, Pecker.

As the day pass, some unanswered questions starts gettin solved. Bart's one of the furst to come to offer his condolences. In the beginnin he's so stunned he almost stuck for words, which is fierce unusual.

Sure, wasn't I fuckin well drinkin wuth him in Healy's last night, til the squad car crawl by an Gillick stick his big nose out, an the boss man cryin, Time up this minute, gents! The guards is outside. An we're outa there in double quick time, I can assure ya, which must be round half-eleven. We talk for a short while on the footpath before goin our separate ways. That's the last I see of poor auld Blocker.

What happen after that? the Puckeen aks. There's a bit of a pause, cause nobody knows.

Well, I might be able to help ye there, says Joe Joe an he just comin intiv the room to offer hus his sympathy. A good friend a mine's walkin past the barracks last night when the squad car pull up at the kerb an out gets the sarge, luggin Blocker after him an hauls him up the steps. He's about to go away when he catch sight of Gillick's shadow appearin on the light-coloured blind. Liftin his baton, he bring it down with all his might on your poor da's head.

That's for yer son humiliating me in front of the Monsignor! he hears him screaming.

It's my fault then? I say.

Not at all, son. The one at fault here, no doubt, is the sarghint.

No wonder he don't come tiv the door this mornin wuth the news, I add.

He send a young stoomer insthead to do his dirty work, says the Puckeen.

Is there any'hin can be done? me ma aks.

Not a fuckin happorth, says Bart.

Hauld aan now, says Joe Joe. Then a huge argument begin.

Won't the doctors in the hospical know what kill him? says the Puckeen.

Sure they will, but they won't tell youse.

What ya mane?

If the sergeant's at fault, there'll be a cover-up. They're definitely not goin to say he was killed by a belt off Gillick's baton. The doctors an the guards they'll all close ranks to protect a member of the law.

Still, I'd like to hear their verdict, says Joe Joe.

Little point in goin tiv the doctor when the patient's dead, me granny mumble.

I tell you what they'll come up wuth before they even start, says Bart. Somethin like death from natural causes or another favourite – death by misadventure. I keep tellin ye only yis won't listen. There'll be a big cover up, folks.

It's bad enough takin away a man's life, says the Puck, but to try an take away his honour as well? That's the least a man ought to be let hauld on to this side of the grave?

Honour is more precious than gold, Joe Joe say.

True, says me gran. Sure what else can anyone keep? I've yet to see a hearse drawin a trailer to the grave.

In this heart here me da's honour's still alive an well, I say, thumpin me chest.

True, an in mine too, son, Bart says blockin a tear.

Truth speaks even tho' the tongue be dead, says me gran.

That sarghint – Jesus, I'll fuckin well choke him, Bart shout as his hands make a pair of very angry fists.

The least that ought be done is file a complaint with the District Superintendent, Joe Joe says.

That be like pissin agin the wind, says Bart.

I sit takin all this in, the anger I tell you about, Pecker, gettin a firm hault in me. She fester an grow in the comin weeks.

Should we try an have the remains removed tiv the cean? me ma aks, bringin events nearer home.

Jesus, maam, you's dead right, says Bart. I'll contact the hospital. I'll be plantin a few words in Gillick's ear too. There's load a things needs answerin. Question Time's about to begin in earnest, folks! At that he get up off his chair an dash out the door about his business.

Isn't he a cruel direct man? Joe Joe whisper rale mild.

He mean well. If there's any root to this, he'll find it, says the Puckeen.

No point in him complainin tiv a man wuth no pity, say me granny.

In one away we's glad Bart's gone for a while, cause he too fond a callin a spade a spade, which upset the women in particular. But that the way he's made.

Joe Joe's a great help workin out plans for the removal. He have a grand calm way tiv him an about the only sane head amongst hus.

Later Bart storm in again wuth bags a cakes an tarts – things he buy in Brady's supermarket – an plonk them on the kitchen table.

Bart you shouldn't a bothered, I say, figurin for the first time that Whackser Joyce, who just turned fifteen, is now wearin the trousers in the cean.

But Bart ignore me. The sarghint isn't available, his stuck-up auld sow of a missus is just after tellin me at the door. By Jesus I gives her a bit of me tongue. Sure every dog in the street knows yer better half assault that poor man, I says.

That's not true, says she. He bang his head off the iron bedstead in his cell. You can see the blood on it if you want.

He'll be hearin a lot more about this, I shout in her ear. Then she slam the door in me face. Next I goes into the hospital to ask about havin the remains returned to the house to be waked, an they refuse. If that isn't a cover up, what is?

Did they tell you why? aks Joe Joe.

Oh the usual excuse – procedure. When they do a post-mortem, they prefer the removal take place from the hospical mortuary after the family view the corpse. That way the public's not able to see the damage that animal done. Anyone here want to see the remains?

I do, I says.

The women in the cean isn't inclined to budge cause they's

findin this all too upsettin. I still believe we should try an have him brought back tiv the house to be waked, me ma insist.

Dead on, says Bart.

I go along with that, says Joe Joe.

# 24

The three of hus pile into Bart's black Ford Consul an before headin for the hospical Bart drive straigh for the undertaker. They stay talkin in his cean for ages. When Bart come out he have a great red face on him. That take care a that, he say to hus without explainin any further.

When we reach the hospical, we's not sure if we be let intiv the morgue. The receptionist isn't too sure neither. She ring a certain doctor an tell him why we's here. Minutes later this auld geezer in a white coat come in.

Bart do the talkin. We'd like to see the remains.

Are ye all relatives of the deceased?

Some of hus is, I say.

Are you not a bit young to be viewing the corpse?

I want to see if it's me da.

He bring hus down a lengthy corridor to a room wuth the name Morgue wrote on the dure. We follow yer man in. Fornenst hus is a body lyin on a trolly covered by a white sheet. I nearly gag when he lift it off the head.

I wouldn't do worse if I war to batter his head in wuth a hammer, the Puckeen say. An all that damage come from a fall?

That's what it says on the death cert.

Who sign it? aks Bart.

Doctor Hoctor.

The shadogs' friend, I hear Joey whisper.

How could a man collect so many bruises from one accidental fall? Bart aks.

Perhaps he was in a fight before he was arrested? How am I to know?

I'd say you know more than yer makin out. I can smell a cover up here.

I can only go by what's on the cert.

Talk about closin ranks, Pecker. Anyway to make a long story short, the undertaker come an after a lot a wranglin we get permission to put me da intiv a coffin an bring him home so we can wake him good an proper in the cean as I'm sure he woulda liked.

There's strong pisherogs among Travellers when it come to havin any'hin to do about dyin, Pecker. People's fierce strict bout where you's suppose to be burrit, an me da bein a Tuam man that where he oughta be reshted, a lot of them is claimin. A big argument get ruz bout it in the cean. Me ma complain it too far to go visit the grave an she have a point there true enough.

The Puckeen say it only right he resht among his own in Galway. Whin me time come, I goin back to Kerry, he say.

Good for you, say me gran. Hope you know someone down there who'll keep the nettles off ya.

In the end we figure it's handier he be reshted in Ballynob Cemetery, but that go agin the grain I can tell ya, Pecker. Nearly all the Joyces that comes to pay their lasht respects keeps wailin, He should be laid in Tuam wuth his own.

This the place we put roots in now, an it only right we lay claim tiv the graveyard the same as ana buffer, says me ma.

The Monsignor, fair dues tiv him, come an pay his last respects too an offer to say the funeral mass.

That kind of ya, says me mother, but I don't know if he'd a been on for that himself, Father, cause he never much of a believer.

Our Lord sacrificed His life for the salvation of all mankind, Missus Joyce.

I not arguin wuth that.

How come the Man above dayle hus such a lousy hand, Father? I aks the cuinnic then.

He didn't make it to suit everyone, lad.

Ya mane He didn't have the likes a hus in mind?

He stop to consider. Then he go off on a different tack entirely. He must take hus for pure eejits or some'hin.

It's the will of God, son – a trial He's puttin your family thro'. Bear up an you'll be rewarded in the next world, providin you lead a good honest life in this one. Out of tragedy an death comes life an truth. It's all part of God's plan.

Any chance He might restore me da's life an make sure the truth be tauld about how he die?

He don't do things that way. Man has free will. That's the reason you've good an bad men in this world. Like I said, it's a test. You get rewarded for the good an punished for the bad in the next life. That's why He send His own son down to teach us how to behave towards one another in this life.

Didn't have any effect on the Grunter an he goin to Mass every mornin.

What you say, son?

For His troubles they nail Him to the cross?

That's right.

Pity they didn't fuckin weld Him tiv it.

What's that you said?

Don't mind him, Father, me ma butt in. He's still very angry over what happen tiv his father.

203

No reason why he should be blaspheemin like that, Missus Joyce.

*

Jesus, some sight a people turn up for the wake too. One thing I notice is all the mutterin an whisperin goin on bout the bruises on me da's head. That an the skin on his face turnin the colour a burnt candlewax make him look a awful sight. Christ, some'hin have to be done about that auld sergeant – that what lots of them's mutterin.

The removal tiv the chapel go handy enough. Monsignor Diskin – fair plays tiv him – does a great job on the prayers an give a fine speech. Hope I get as good a send off up the road, Pecker.

After that a large group goes tiv the pub. The shadogs stays away from the scene. Suppose they know better. That night instead of the crowd goin away about its business, it seem to get bigger. Travellers is comin in from all parts for the funeral tomorrow. It's a very heartenin sight, Pecker, an it warm the cockles of me heart to see how me da be so popular.

The funeral next mornin is huge an it all go grand an peaceful. Afterward the pubs does a fierce trade agin. Whin it come tiv evenin, though, things start to get tricky. The traipe bring out a lot of anger in the tribes. Closin time come an lots of them doesn't want to leave. Next thing the shadogs makes a showin an that's like a red rag tiv a bull. One of me da's cousints starts mouthin, What we goin to do bout that sarghint, lads?

A gang of them form out on the street. A fight start. Extra shadogs is brought in from Mullingar an Marboro. There's no sight at all of the Grunter.

A pitched battle rage for at least a hour. Sticks, stones,

any'hin that come to hand gets flung. Cars, windies, any'hin that get in the way is smashed. It kinda remind ya what the blacks do later on up in the Sixties, Pecker. That night we's way ahead of our time in them regards.

Next thing there's a baton charge. Heads gets badly bashed an many Travellers gets pegged intiv the Black Marias they has waitin an is druve away.

Fair dues tiv our crowd. They let the guards know how we feel about what the Grunter do tiv me da. Still the shadogs clear the streets an the followin day every'hin is back to normal. The townies is doin fierce complainin bout the tinkers an the damage they do. No word at all about Gillick an the way he murder me father.

Auld traditions die hard, Pecker, an me granny – fair plays tiv her – make sure they's followed to the full. We'll sthart wuth his caravan, she say a few days after he's burrit.

All his clothes gets pegged in – any'hin that belong tiv him – his pipes, tobaccy, caubeens, photos even. The very door knobs in the cean is knocked off an thrun in too. Poor auld Eyebrowser, his special dog, is put down an placed on top of his clothes inside.

One night the Puckeen come round wuth the van an haul the whole lot out tiv the Heath to a nice quiet spot. We all go along wuth him.

I sprinkle petrol on the flure of the caravan. He light a torch an hand it tiv me. We stand well back while I peg it in the dure. There's a great whoopin sound an up she go – flames lightin up the sky. We stand watchin for ages til nothin's left only a black twisted heap of aluminium on a metal frame lyin on a smoulderin bed of embers.

A terrible waste a good money, Goat complains in me ear.

Yer da, an every'hin belongin tiv him is well an truly gone now, says me gran.

All but the memories, I say.

They'll fade too.

Not wuth me they won't! I cry wuth tears in me eyes.

The soul go out of me after me da's death, Pecker. I go round in a daze. I turn in on meself. Any time I sees the sarghint, I feel nothin but raw burnin hate. This man ruin our lives an he's not finished wuth hus yet, I fear. He waitin a little while for things to settle fore he come after hus agin.

Be Jesus, you not goin to let him get away wuth this, is ya? this divil inside me keep sayin. Is there no justice at all in the world? Bart keep arguin there's nothin anyone can do an he know. Sure they is the law, he say.

I'm too upset to take the fox over tiv Hennessy for to collect the reward. Instead, me an Joe Joe takes her up tiv the mountain in the cage an set her free in the heather of the Glenbarrow Valley where we hope she be safe.

A month pass. I still feel no better. Noddy get on tiv me in the hotel to pull out of it.

I say tiv him, If it war yer father, mevvy you'd feel different, ya bollix.

I give up goin to school. Whin I sees Sally up the road, I drop me head an turn the other way. It all because of them nightmares I be havin, Pecker – doin in me head – especially the one wuth the Grunter an them gritty teeth an sweaty face, smashin down the baton wuth all his might, time an time again, on me poor auld dad's nopper.

Snap out of it! says the fella in me head.

Only whin you get your own back, the divil in me is sayin.

One day I is workin out in Creeper's whin I make up me mind.

*

She mighty busy out there, Noddy say tiv me this night in the hotel.

That's cause of the novena, I answer.

One porterhouse an onions for our friend, Noddy call.

No arse wipe this time, Pecker. This call for stronger medicine. She's slapped intiv the sizzlin pan an took out medium rare. Waitin for the onions, I pull out me little syringe an inject a little squart of the quare stuff intiv the meat.

In all his innocence, Noddy place the plate in front of him. While he eatin it, he make the odd quare face, but his huge appetite make him too greedy to want to stop.

Afterward he wash the strange taste outa his mouth wuth a rake a pints in the bar. It only whin he gettin into bed that he start to get this cruel burnin in his throat an belly. Sure I musht a give him about a teaspoon of the tack. Anyway he get rushed tiv the hospical where they pump him out but divil a good it do. I hear after the pain he go thro' is nothin short of extraordinary. They end up anointin the auld fucker. Still he wouldn't die. He come out bout a year later a shadow of his rale self, his nerves in tatters. He have to retire from the force. Whatever the poison do, it give the caideog Auldtimer's disease an he die bout two year later.

It don't take them too long to find out who destroy the Grunter. Jesus, I'm hauled in an any'hin like the corripin I get. Well they bate me black an blue, Pecker. Nor was I exactly the flavour of the month in the auld helm. Even Bart turn his back on me, but Joe Joe, fair plays tiv him, he stay friendly an often visit me in later years.

As for Sally, I say she come under cruel pressure from her

auld wan, but she turn her back on me too. Next thing I hear she go to England.

The day they lock me up inside, Pecker, me auld head really start reelin. I just can't stand to be hemmed in. Even in the helm I feel trapped, so you can imagine what it like to be thrun inside an they throw away the key!

The furst kip they put me in is Daingean Reformatory. I meet this tough fella from Dublin be the name a Cahill an I aks him the best way a gettin kicked outa this hole. He tell me what they really hate is if ya start settin fire to things. One day this brother start feelin me in the kitchen. That night I pour paraffin on his bed an set fire to it. The fire brigade get called in an they have a mighty job stoppin the whole place from goin up.

Them priests an brothers gives me a fierce beatin over that an I get thrun intiv St Pat's in Dublin. Some kip that was, Pecker. Again I get cruel pissed off. One night the same thing – I set fire tiv a store room. Before I know it I gets pegged intiv Dundrum, the place where the head-the-balls goes.

They starts feedin me all colours a pills there to calm me down but they don't do much good. Then they start injectin me wuth different kinds a michemicals. They even give me lectric shock treatment. It's a miracle I've anthin left upstairs after all them years a rabusin, Pecker.

I get bounced round intiv different places then an before I know it one decade borrow another. There's no way they goin to forgive ya for killin a shadog, specially a auld magarlach of a sarghint.

It's while I'm in Daingean that a shower from the town burns down our house, an then the Puckeen's one night shortly after. It's a pure miracle no one's kilt.

Afterward both families moves to Dublin. There's not much more I can tell ya, Peck. Sure ya know the rest.

Now isn't that a mighty tale an every word of it true! Sure why wouldn't it, an it me last confession on this earth? An all this happen in the space of about four month. It screw up me whole life – gettin bounced round from one place tiv another like a yo-yo til they finally let me out a few year ago all dressed up an washed out with nowhere to go.

\*

I didn't realise it at the time but this was to be my last session with my uncle. During the following week he became incoherent.

Before I left that evening an amazing event occurred, proving the adage that truth is stranger than fiction. In fact I would have to classify this as a minor miracle – the biggest cliché in this whole biography.

I was putting away my tape recorder when a knock came on the door. Two women entered. One looked young enough to be the other's daughter and she was holding a baby in her arms.

I could see Whack's eyes light up.

Sally! he cried at the elder.

Your brother Eaney told me in England, Sally said. I've brought your daughter and grandson along.

What ya mane?

Remember the evenin the she-fox was watchin?

Jesus, I don't believe this!

You got me pregnant. This is your daughter, Jacqueline.

She was the spitting image of her dad. Tall and slim with curly blond hair and pretty – she rested her son on the bed beside him.

What's his name?

We've already enough Jacks in the family, so we called him John. She spoke in a distinct cockney accent.

I didn't wish to intrude any further and left them to themselves. I bid them goodbye – proud to be part of the travelling tribe, even though I was out on a limb. But fair play to them. One has to admire the way they showed loyalty and respect for one of their own on his deathbed.

I departed knowing my uncle was tingling with the greatest surprise he could ever possibly receive.

It couldn't have come at a more appropriate time too in what was left of his short life, for barring another miracle, Whack wasn't going to be with us much longer.

He had many callers to his bedside to offer him comfort after that. In reality they were coming to pay their last respects.

One week later on the fourteenth of September 1998 my Uncle Whack died. He lies in Ballynob cemetery next to his father and mother.

# Glossary of Cant and Colloquial English Words

baluba: berserk
ballyragger: braggart
banners: potatoes, chips
beor: woman
bile: boil
budget: toolbox
buffer: country person
buffsham: countrified townie
burrit: buried
caideog: bollix
cakesham: coarse-mannered
  townie
cant: traveller's language
carnish: meat
childer: children
cean: house
chuck: food
clem: spoil
cob: cabbage
cuinnic: priest
conie: rabbit
corrip: beat
cream cracker: cockney for
  knacker
creeper: cat
cuckoots: cahoots
cullions: potatoes
curra: horse
curdles: curls
cuter: coax
dale: deal
do-bar: assault
deener: money

dreeper: bottle
dudgeen: pipe
dure: door
edificatin: education
feen: travelling man
flure: floor
fore: before
fornenst: in front of
forkin: fortune
fountie: water
gallery: fun
furst: first
gat: porter
garaid: money
gat-cean: public-house
geezer: cunning person
girdle: girl
glimmer: fire
gloak: look
gomadoodle: fool
gom or gomey: fool
graipe: fork
grade: money
grunter: pig
hauld: hold
helm: town
hus, husses: us
larrup: hit or beat
lind: lend
lurog   eye
lush: drink
magarlach: bollix
mate: meat

Marboro: Portlaoise
marrit: married
meider: annoy
mevvy: maybe
michemicals: chemicals
mideog: money
minceir: traveller
minic: name
molly: camp
monicker: name
mooch: beg
muog: pig
Mulchas: Thomas
mush: Co Offaly person
nark: steal
nopper: head
oglers: eyes
pavee: traveller
peck: food
pisherogs: superstitions
pog: kiss
pragg: heavy workhorse
rabuse: abuse
Ribleen: Brigid
roomogs: eggs
ruz: rose

ruilla: mad
shadog: garda
snazzy wazzy: snobbish
sham: settled man
skyhope: whiskey
spike: hospital
steamers: cigarettes
stoomer: fool
streagale    bottle
swallas: swallows
thrun: thrown
tiv: to
tome: good
tober: road
trimmers: sticks
turmics: turnips
ushta: used to
traipe: alcoholic drink
war: was
waxie: lino
windie: window
wide: in the know
wuth: with

## Phrases and Sayings

lush your gricheir: eat your
    dinner
jump the budget: get married
get below the bottom board:
    get inside someone's mind
gladar box: a money making
    machine

notorious knat: gallant rogue
pucks of: lots of
ruilla builla: ructions
tutter maloga: sexual
    intercourse
the faithful county:
    County Offaly